Books by Kathleen Pennell

Pony Investigator Series
The Case of the Missing Money
The Case of the Phantom Stallion
The Case of the Midnight Stranger
The Case of the Mysterious Circus
The Case of the Secret Passage
The Case of the Mirror Image

The Adventures In Time Series
The Door into Time
Rescued in Time

Lancelot Maddox Series
The Boy on the Bench
Ragtag Rescue
The Missing Agent
Plane Down

A Treadwell Mystery Series
The Face in the Water
The Man at the Ruins

PADDOCK
PUBLISHING
Lancaster Pennsylvania

LANCELOT MADDOX SERIES
BOOK 2

Ragtag
Rescue
and other stories

KATHLEEN PENNELL

www.kathleenpennell.com

Table of Contents

Ragtag Rescue

It had been a long week for Lancelot Maddox. He had tests to study for and worked overtime at the intelligence agency where he was a part-time decoder. He planned on an early bedtime that night. But trouble was brewing six thousand miles away that would rob him of that sleep.

Undercover Agent Fillmore sat on a park bench late in the afternoon when it was crowded with people. Fillmore was his code name. Very few people knew his real name. He flicked open his newspaper and pretended to read but his ears were alert for the sound of familiar footsteps. The double agent he'd recruited in this country, not too friendly to his own, had signaled that he urgently needed to see him. There was critical information that could not wait. He was paid very handsomely to deliver information, but then he also risked his life to do it. Fillmore checked his watch as he turned the page. The double agent was late.

There was that ever-present fear that the double agent had been caught. If that happened, Fillmore had a planned path of escape for both of them that he hoped they'd never have to use. With each passing minute, the worry grew. Perspiration collected on the sides of his face but his hands remained steady.

Twenty minutes later, the familiar footsteps approached walking more rapidly than usual. The other man also carried a newspaper.

"You're late," Fillmore said quietly without moving his lips.

"Two men were following me. I had to lose them first otherwise they'd arrest both of us."

Fillmore swallowed hard but maintained his composure. "When did they become suspicious?"

"Last week," he said. "I'm leaving the country as soon as our meeting is over. This will be the last time I see you."

"I understand," Fillmore said feeling a tightening in his stomach wondering if they were both being watched as they sat there. "Why did you call this meeting? What information have you got for me?"

"First, did you bring the money? I need it to get away."

"I brought it," Fillmore said then shifted slightly revealing a thick packet.

Highly experienced, the double agent managed to slip it into his pocket while retrieving a handkerchief. "There's a traitor at your intelligence agency leaking information to my government. I only found out about it last night," the double agent said.

Fillmore was silent for a moment as his mind adjusted to the fact that the traitor may be someone he knew. "You sure?"

"I'm sure."

"I need a name."

"Don't have a name."

"How high up is the traitor?" Fillmore said. "All the way to the Chief?"

"No, I'd know if it was your Chief. I don't know who the traitor is. All I know is there is one."

As Fillmore slowly turned the page of his newspaper, his eyes swept the immediate area but saw nothing that might indicate they were being watched. "What do you know about the traitor?"

"Nothing except two agents are flying out tomorrow morning to pick up classified information from him."

"You used the word 'him'," Fillmore said. "So the traitor is a man."

"Yes, but that's all I know."

"Why do they have to fly there?" Fillmore said. "Can't they get the information without leaving the country?"

"That's the only way the traitor will do business."

"He's probably afraid of delivering the information and not getting paid," Fillmore said. "What time does their flight take off?"

"Ten o'clock. It's the only airline flying to your country at ten. They'll board separately and sit apart."

"Of course, I'd expect that."

"How will I know who the agents are?" Fillmore said.

"I couldn't risk bringing photos or any information about them with me. Yesterday, after I called you, I put everything I had on them in the drop location I've used before to deliver papers."

9

"All right, I'll pick it up after I leave here."

The double agent left first walking in the opposite direction from which he came.

Agent Fillmore waited ten minutes while he made plans. He needed to talk to Biggs at the intelligence agency. Biggs was a retired army intelligence officer currently employed by the agency as head of security. He could trust Biggs but he needed more information first.

Agent Fillmore spent a restless, fearful night then took the same flight as the foreign agents sitting several rows behind them. They sat across from each other, didn't speak, and gave the impression they were total strangers. When the plane landed, both men picked up separate cars rented for them in advance.

Agent Fillmore was challenged with the task of which one to follow. In the final analysis, it made no difference because, even though they had separate cars and left the airport in different direction, they met at the same location.

Fillmore grabbed a taxi and followed one of them. He asked the driver to keep a car between him and the car he was following hoping the foreign agent wouldn't sense he was being tailed. When the car pulled into a vacant warehouse, the driver dropped Fillmore off at the next block. The agent kept to the side of the narrow road and walked back thankful it was a moonless night. He made a quick call to the intelligence agency and asked for Biggs. But the head of security wouldn't arrive for another hour.

The two foreign agents were also highly experienced. They knew how to skillfully tail someone. They also knew when someone was tailing them. So it concerned Agent Fillmore that, even with all his experience as an agent, the two men may suspect they were being followed from the time they boarded the plane until they reached the warehouse. He had to put his faith in his years of training and experience hoping they were still unaware of his existence.

The two men were in the warehouse for twenty minutes when Fillmore decided to slip around to the back of the building. What he saw confirmed the double agent's claims. There was a car parked in the back. He watched as the two men unloaded its contents and took them into the building. Why were they doing that? It seemed completely backwards. If their intent was to steal classified information, why not drive away with it? And why hadn't the material been microfilmed rather than deal with these bulky files? Unless, they wanted to inspect the merchandise first, then microfilm what they wanted, and leave the country with it hidden somewhere. It was a puzzle he couldn't solve without more information.

He walked to the other side of the building and cut a hole into the window just above the latch. The window hadn't been opened in decades. It was a huge warehouse. If he knew exactly where the two men were stationed, it would save everyone time when the backup arrived. He made his way soundlessly through the empty building until he came to a door with light shining under it.

Fillmore left the same way he came. He needed to talk to Biggs but would the night duty officer transfer the call to him or want more information first. If that happened, he'd have to come up with a likely story or hope the person who answered the phone was not the traitor. He needed backup immediately. It was a chance he had to take.

At three o'clock in the morning, he called the intelligence agency. "This is Fillmore," he said. "Who's this?"

"Ted Rader. Night-duty officer."

"I need to speak to Biggs."

"He's making rounds of the building so he's not in his office."

"When will be in his office?"

"Fifteen minutes," Rader said.

Fillmore hesitated but he needed help. "Look, Rader. There's been a break in security."

"How bad is it?"

"It's bad. I need to talk to Biggs or Chief."

"Chief is out of the country at a high-level meeting. He can't be reached. Maybe I can help you."

"How high is your security clearance?"

"I'm the night-duty officer so obviously I'm cleared for classified information."

"Two foreign agents are holed up a block away from me." Fillmore hesitated. "There's been a significant amount of activity since I got here. They may pack up and leave any minute, so we need to move in quickly. I need backup. Get a few people you know well and trust. I'll wait until you get here." He gave Rader the address and then silence weighed heavily.

"You still there?" Rader asked.

"There's a traitor somewhere in the agency," Fillmore said.

Rader felt his muscles tense. "A traitor? You sure?"

"I'm positive."

"Do you know who it is?"

"No idea, but one exists. I took a chance and slipped inside the warehouse so I know where they're holed up. I'll be two blocks west of the building waiting for you. Don't bring anyone you wouldn't trust with your life. Even someone you trust with your life may be the traitor."

"Understood. Hang in there, Fillmore," Rader said. "I'll be there as fast as I can pull a team together."

Having assembled a list of agents, the night duty officer walked down the hall to Mr. Biggs' office to brief him on the phone call he'd received. Rader explained in a very few words the nature of the phone call, then said, "Look, Biggs, it's critical I join Fillmore immediately. You brief the people on this list and tell them where to meet me. Got it?"

Mr. Biggs ran his eyes down the list of familiar names. "No problem. I'll take care of it."

"What's happening cannot be made public. Nobody, and I mean nobody, outside the agency must find out." The duty officer's eyes darted around the small office for a moment before he continued, "I'm not sure what we're facing here. Either Fillmore's got it all wrong or there's been a serious breach in security."

Mr. Biggs entered the code to open the front door then stood aside while the duty officer bolted through it. The door was nearly closed when he heard a car scream around the corner and screech to a halt. He stood by helplessly as two men manhandled the duty officer into the car then sped away. He ran down the steps, but the car's lights were off and it was dark. Identifying the vehicle was impossible.

After retracing his steps, Mr. Biggs gazed down the long, empty hallway. Setting his mouth in a firm line, he sat at his desk and worked his way down the list of agents. Each call went directly to voicemail. What were the odds that every phone was turned off? And there was something in the voicemail messages that added mystery and urgency to the situation. He eased back in his chair. If none of the agents were available, who could he contact? There was one employee whose name wasn't on the list. He wasn't an agent, but he was trustworthy.

Lancelot Maddox was dog-tired. He sifted through his blurry brain for a word that meant "beyond exhaustion". Perhaps he'd coin a word and his name would appear in the dictionary. How about "elephant-tired" or even "whale-tired"?

Two major tests and working an hour overtime every day at his after-school decoding job at the intelligence agency had precipitated this burned-out feeling. With no time to study at school, he was up until midnight preparing for tests, which he probably failed on a spectacular level. By ten o'clock, he struggled up to his bedroom with his backpack thudding against every step. He pulled on sweatpants and a t-shirt, leaving his school clothes piled in a heap on the floor, then collapsed into bed.

An irritating, persistent noise broke through the cavern of his sleep. With his eyes closed and his brows furrowed, Lancelot patted around the top of his nightstand, knocking his cell phone onto the floor. Hanging over the edge of the bed, he drew the phone to his ear. "Hello," he croaked.

"Kid?"

"Who's this?" Lancelot asked groggily.

"Biggs. Security Division."

"Mr. Biggs?" Lancelot said. He put on his glasses and looked at his clock. "It's three-thirty in the morning!"

"Called everyone else. Nobody is available. It's down to you and me, kid."

"Does a message have to be decoded right now? Can't it wait until tomorrow? I mean later today?"

"Not about decoding, kid. I know where the problem is, and we've got to be there in twenty minutes."

"Twenty minutes?" Lancelot murmured. He rolled onto his back while the cell phone began to slip from his hand.

"Pick you up in ten," Mr. Biggs said. "Got a gun?"

Lancelot's eyes flew open. "A what? A gun? Did you just ask me if I have a gun?"

"I did."

Lancelot sat up. "Well, uh, no. We don't keep—I mean, I don't know anything about guns."

"Can't be helped. I'll do the nasty work if it comes to that."

"You don't mean what I think you mean, do you?" Lancelot stammered, then asked hastily, "What does Chief have to say about this? Did you call him? Maybe he can find somebody else to go with you."

"Out of the country?"

"Chief is out of the country?! I just saw him yesterday afternoon at work."

"Emergency. Came up at the last minute. High-security meeting. Tried but couldn't reach him."

"Well, well," Lancelot said, desperately searching for an escape hatch. "I'm only a decoder. And only part time. You haven't forgotten that, have you?"

"Not likely, kid. I let you in the building three times each week at three-thirty."

"Why don't you call one of the agents I see floating around down there? This is their job, not mine."

"Nobody answered. Calls went to voicemail."

"Well, what about the night-duty officer? Somebody's supposed to be there around the clock."

"Tell you about him later."

"Mr. Biggs. I'm only fourteen years old. You know that, right? I mean, isn't there some kind of age requirement about going on life-threatening assignments in the middle of the night? And another thing. I'm the smallest kid in my entire class. I couldn't wrestle a flea to the ground."

"Look, kid. If you're not up to it, I'll go it alone."

Lancelot swung his legs over the side of the bed, cradling his head with his free hand. "I didn't—I mean, I wouldn't want you to deal with whatever this is alone and get hurt," he said lamely.

"Good. Be there in ten minutes. Wear dark clothes," Mr. Biggs said then ended the call.

Ten minutes? Dark clothes? At three-thirty in the morning! He'd been on several missions with Mr. Biggs before but never in the middle of the night. It was unsettling being awakened only to be told to wear dark clothes and did he have a gun. He muttered a stream of useless phrases he should have said as he stumbled across the room. He whipped out one of his oversized black t-shirts. He'd begged his mother to buy the smallest men's shirts she could find then shrink them in the dryer. This one was still too big, but at least the label proved he'd surpassed kid's clothes.

He eased down the stairs carrying his shoes, avoiding the steps that creaked, agonizing over the fact that sneaking out of the safety of the family home was the least of his worries. Slipping out the front door without being heard was his next challenge. Did the door squeak? Funny how you don't notice things like that when it doesn't matter.

Seconds later, Mr. Biggs ground to a halt. His brakes were loud enough to wake the entire neighborhood. He waited two seconds while Lancelot launched onto the passenger seat, pulling the rusted door shut with both hands. Mr. Biggs shoved his foot on the accelerator and the truck hopped forward, angrily belching smoke out of the exhaust.

Lancelot patted around on the right side of his seat, then turned to Mr. Biggs. "You still don't have seatbelts?" He was fairly certain he was about to preach a lesson on the safety of seatbelts. "Do you know how many lives seatbelts save?"

"No," Mr. Biggs said. "Do you?"

"Well, no, but really you should have seatbelts in your truck. They could save your life, and how about mine?"

"Look, kid, I've been through more dangerous stuff than you'll ever face in your entire life."

Lancelot studied the head of security with interest. Just what did Mr. Biggs mean by "dangerous stuff"? Was he exaggerating? He knew nothing about the head of security's past life except he was an army intelligence officer for thirty years before coming to work at the intelligence agency.

As they wheeled around the next corner, Lancelot grabbed the arm rest on the door for support. When it broke loose in his hands, he placed it on the floor, careful to avoid letting it slide through the jagged hole between his feet. With nothing else in sight, he gripped what was left of the dashboard. Houses flew past his window. He glanced sideways at the speedometer. It registered zero. Figures!

Lancelot pushed his glasses farther up on his nose. "Where are we going? And what's this all about?"

"Somebody messing around with our system."

"Kids do stuff like that all the time," Lancelot said, relaxing just a hair. "They'll fold as soon as we walk through the door."

"Don't think so. Only professionals could have penetrated the level of security system, encryption, and anti-theft defenses we have."

"Professionals hacked into our system?" Lancelot turned horrified eyes to the head of security. "When did it happen?"

"Not sure. Ted Rader just found out."

"The night-duty officer?"

"Right."

"How'd he find out?" Lancelot said.

"Got a call from an undercover agent."

"But how did he find out?"

"Don't know yet. Hope to find out when we get there," Mr. Biggs said.

"Okay," Lancelot said, then remembered something Mr. Biggs had said on the phone. "What were you going to tell me about Mr. Rader?"

The head of security hesitated before saying, "Kidnapped."

Lancelot's mouth dropped open. "Kidnapped?! What do you mean kidnapped?"

"I let him out the front door. Car rounded the corner and two men grabbed him."

Lancelot was pretty sure his heart stopped beating. His breathing certainly had. "Did you see who it was? Did you call the police?"

"No and no."

Lancelot turned in his seat. "Why not?!"

"Undercover mission, kid. Need-to-know basis only."

"And the police don't need to know?!"

"Got my orders, kid." Mr. Biggs looked at Lancelot with a raised eyebrow. "Police don't need to know. At least not at this point."

"Mr. Rader couldn't have known he'd be kidnapped! You should have called the police."

"Inter-agency problem," the head of security said firmly. "We'll take care of it."

Lancelot laid his head in his trembling hands, then looked up. In two minutes, his mind had shifted from "kids" to "professionals" hacking into their system, then kidnapping the night-duty officer. "Do the hackers know everything we've decoded this week?"

"No idea."

"What about the agents?" Lancelot said. "They're supposed to be available. How could they let their calls go to voicemail?"

Mr. Biggs shook his head, his mouth forming a straight line.

19

"Why are you shaking your head?" Lancelot said, with growing alarm. "What happened?"

"All the calls went straight to voicemail."

Lancelot waited several seconds, then said, "Straight to voicemail? You mean their phones didn't even ring?"

"Not even once."

"They're not supposed to turn off their phones, are they?"

Mr. Biggs shook his head. "Against regulations."

When Mr. Biggs didn't elaborate, Lancelot said, "Is there something you're not telling me?"

"Every single recording had the same voice and the same message."

"The same?" Lancelot whispered, then said loudly, "You mean it was some kind of computer-generated response, like 'sorry, I'm not available', that kind of thing?"

Mr. Biggs glanced sideways. "No. Nothing like that."

"What did the message say?"

"They all said, 'You're wasting your time'."

Lancelot felt like the wind had just been knocked out of him, like the time he tripped on the soccer field and landed squarely on the ball. "'You're wasting your time'?" he said, his voice trembling. "Right to voicemail with the same voice and the same message for everyone." He thought about this a moment. "They set this whole thing up ahead of time."

Mr. Biggs nodded approvingly. "Didn't take you long to figure it out, kid."

Lancelot figured out the next part, too. "If they set up the voicemail

20

ahead of time, they may know we're coming and be waiting for us. Did you think of that?"

"Of course I thought of that."

"What are we going to do if half a dozen criminals are waiting for us?"

Mr. Biggs patted the gun laying on the seat between them.

Lancelot closed his eyes and rested his head against the side window, which was a mistake. Within ten seconds he had a headache from the unrelenting vibrations. "We can't just shoot our way in there."

"I never shoot my way into anything, kid."

Lancelot eyed the head of security. It positively defied logic where this older, slightly built man got his self-confidence. Obviously there was a side to Mr. Biggs he didn't know and may never find out. "What are we going to do when we get there?"

"Figure that out when I know what we're facing."

"But you know where it's happening, don't you? That's where we're heading, right?"

"Empty warehouse, east end of town. Know where I mean?"

Lancelot's eyes doubled. "There?!"

"Yes, there."

"That's not a very nice place to be this time of night. Actually, that's not a very nice place to be during the daytime either."

"Can't pick where the action is, kid," Mr. Biggs said, then added in a rare moment of elucidation, "We'll ease up to the warehouse and have a look-see. Reconnaissance. Then we'll have a better idea what we're facing."

"I understand what you're saying, but how are we going to do that?" Lancelot shouted over the roar of the truck's engine. "They'll hear us coming."

"We won't park right outside the door, kid," Mr. Biggs said, glancing pityingly at Lancelot. "We'll park two blocks away. Approach the warehouse on the dark side of the street so we can see what we're facing before we take any action."

He needn't have worried about being heard. The truck heaved its last, grinding to a lurching halt four blocks from the warehouse. All efforts to restart the clunker came to nothing. The overused, overrated truck was history.

Not skipping a beat, Mr. Biggs effortlessly turned to the next page. He stuck his gun in the back of his trousers and shoved open the door. "Okay, kid. Time to earn our pay."

"I'm getting paid for this?"

"Turn of phrase, kid. Might find anything. Stay quiet and stay close." While Mr. Biggs moved silently forward, Lancelot trailed close behind.

Suddenly, the head of security stopped and Lancelot pulled up short. There was a small car parked two blocks from their destination, without so much as a hint of another car in the entire area. The strange thing was that it was pulled off the street into a dead-end lane under a tree with limbs covering it, so that only the trunk was visible.

Mr. Biggs walked past the lane, studied the area then doubled back, bending low before making his way to the car. He looked through the back-seat window, then worked his way to the front. He eyed the interior and reached for the handle. It was unlocked. He soundlessly opened it while Lancelot peeked over his shoulder. A man began to slide out, but the head of security caught him before he hit the ground. Balancing the man in one arm, he took out his flashlight and shined it on his face, then sighed. That kind of sigh, for anyone else, would have amounted to a blood-curdling scream.

Lancelot cleared his throat. When he was fairly positive his voice was under control, he said, "Is he…"

After a brief examination, Biggs shook his head as he smoothed back the man's hair. "No, he's still alive. He's been drugged heavily though."

"Drugged?"

"Given something to make him sleep. Looks like they gave him a fairly large dose, too."

"Shouldn't we call for an ambulance?" Lancelot said.

Mr. Biggs placed two fingers on the man's neck checking for a pulse then listened to him breathe. "He'll be all right. Have a whopping headache," he said, gently laying the man on his side.

"Do you know who he is?"

Mr. Biggs nodded. "Code name is Fillmore."

"Fillmore? Was he with the guy who called the night-duty officer?"

"Right. He's the undercover agent who called tonight. I don't think there is anyone else who knows about the security leak but him and the night duty officer who took the call."

"How do you know who he is? I thought undercover agents didn't come into the office," Lancelot said.

"Comes in late at night every few months to see Chief. I let him in through the backdoor. Doesn't take the elevator. Uses the back stairs."

"I don't understand. What's he doing here?"

"He discovered certain information and was following up on it. He called Rader tonight asking for backup. Told him where he was and that he'd be here waiting for everyone to show up. Except nobody showed up in time to help him."

"So, Fillmore is the undercover agent who called the night-duty officer and said to meet him at a certain location," Lancelot said. "Since the bad guys found him first, what's to prevent the same thing from happening to us? And what if nobody shows up to rescue us either? All the agents are asleep, so we'll be next. It's probably a trap and we'll end up just like Fillmore—or worse."

Mr. Biggs ignored Lancelot while he searched the glove compartment. He reached under the passenger-side seat and stretched beyond Agent Fillmore to probe under the driver's-side seat. Finally, he opened the backdoor, climbed inside, giving that area a thorough search. He drew out a slip of paper stuck between the seats, shined his flashlight on it, and stuffed it into an inside pocket of his jacket. Pressing his lips together, he quickly shut the door. "Worried something like this would happen."

Lancelot knew this meant something big but couldn't quite nail down what it was. "What do you mean?"

"Tell you later," Mr. Biggs said, then glanced at Lancelot with a look that said, "Don't ask any more questions."

They continued down the street, but all too soon, the dreaded warehouse loomed ahead shrouded in darkness.

"It's dark. I wonder if they left," Lancelot said.

"Maybe. Maybe not." Mr. Biggs inched forward, aiming for the west side of the warehouse. Their footsteps softened as they drew closer to the building. Pressing against the wall, he studied the dripping face of his sidekick. "You all right?"

"I don't know. I feel kinda funny."

"You'll get used to it."

"I will?" Lancelot said, then added, "I hope I don't have to."

The twinkle in Mr. Biggs' eyes appeared and faded in a microsecond. "Windows might be painted over. Let's check for cracks." Slipping around the corner, he edged up to the first window.

"See anything?" Lancelot whispered.

"No."

They moved quickly from window to window until they came to a door. Mr. Biggs soundlessly turned the handle. Surprisingly, the door was unlocked and he opened it a fraction. "Turning on the flashlight," he whispered. "Be prepared for anything. We may need to make a fast getaway if there's a lot more of them than there are of us."

Lancelot straightened his glasses and steeled himself for the worst.

Mr. Biggs eased open the door and they squeezed through. The darkness was impenetrable. The flashlight swung slowly from area to area. The room was small, probably a reception area in better times. They stood listening but heard nothing coming from the next room. There was a sliver of light slipping under the nearest door and they approached it soundlessly.

Mr. Biggs drew out his gun and whispered, "Wait here. If I'm captured, get out and call the police." When Lancelot's eyebrows rose, he added, "Just tell them a fight broke out. Nothing else. Got it?" Lancelot must have nodded, because in the next second the head of security slowly turned the handle and kicked open the door.

Lancelot waited and listened hoping the worst wouldn't come to pass. Mr. Biggs returned, motioned with his head and Lancelot followed him into a brightly lit room with chipped paint on the walls and cracked linoleum on the floor. Several boxes partially filled with equipment were scattered across the floor. "What's happening?"

"It's possible that the foreign agents are sorting through the material looking for something important enough to microfilm," Mr. Biggs said. "Or they know their cover has been blown and they're making a hasty retreat. Odds are they're boxing up things in preparation for leaving. Don't know where they are or how long they'll be gone, so we need to move quickly," Mr. Biggs said, then glanced at Lancelot. "Look around. See if you recognize anything."

Lancelot made a quick study of the room. There were two computers and two short stacks of papers held together with large clips. Dust had collected around the computers so they'd been there for a while but who had set them up? "The computers have passwords to open them, and I doubt if I'd recognize what I'm looking at anyway."

"Just try. Maybe they're in such a hurry they got sloppy."

Lancelot was an insignificant cog in a huge wheel and was absolutely positive he'd find nothing that looked even remotely familiar. Even so, he sat at the first computer. As he anticipated, he couldn't get beyond the password required to gain access to what was inside. Oddly enough, at the second computer, the previous user was in such a hurry to leave that he left the computer wide open for discovery. Lancelot's eyes raced across the screen as he noted familiar messages he'd decoded earlier in the week. That jarred him to the core. When he hit the first wall which required a password to gain entry, he stood on legs that were none too steady.

He stepped to a table which held two stacks of papers bound together with large clips. He leafed through them noting that a few of them were copies of messages he'd decoded in the past two weeks at the intelligence agency. Lancelot printed out messages to be decoded because it was easier for him to decode using a pencil. Chief didn't object to this practice because once he decoded them and placed them in the night-duty officer's inbox, it was the officer's duty to decide what to do with them.

"Some of these are messages I decoded in the past two weeks," he said softly, then looked at several more sheets which identified agents' names and locations and other vital information. "What if they sell this stuff to somebody we don't like?" Mr. Biggs' reaction mystified him, which is to say there wasn't any. "Why aren't you surprised?"

"They aren't here just to get cell phone numbers." The words had barely settled when they heard the front door open and close in the reception room. Lancelot followed Mr. Biggs behind the door they'd just walked through and waited. Seconds later, three towering men burst through.

When someone spoke, Lancelot's brows furrowed. The voice was familiar, but he couldn't place it. The revelation didn't arrive with lightning speed. It was more of a slow dawning. It was Mr. Rader, the night-duty officer. Their paths had crossed this week only because he had worked one hour overtime.

"Two more trips should do it," Rader said, over the crashing of things being tossed into boxes. "We may not have much more time. Old Biggs won't reach anyone by phone, but you never know with that old guy. When he can't contact anybody by phone, he may actually leave the building and knock on somebody's door. The old fool."

For the first time, Lancelot stopped thinking of himself and looked up at Mr. Biggs. Obviously Ted Rader didn't really know him and had vastly underrated "the old fool". You'd think the head of security would be stiff-lipped with indignation and come out fighting mad. But there he stood, twinkling with a thin smile on his lips.

Mr. Biggs pressed his finger to his lips and pulled out his gun from the back of his trousers. He peered through the slivered opening where the door was hinged to the wall and waited until their backs were turned. Quickly, he slipped past Lancelot and out from behind the door. When none of the men turned, he took a position in the doorway, as if he'd just arrived. "Kidnapping was a nice touch," he said softly.

Silence hung while the three men whirled, saw the man, then saw the gun. Rader barely skipped a beat before saying, "Didn't see your truck outside. How'd you get here?"

Lancelot placed his eye against the crack of the door and waited for Mr. Biggs to make his big move.

Mr. Biggs ignored his question. "What happened to the kidnappers?"

Ted Rader glanced beyond the head of security's shoulder as he gave a short laugh. "Clumsy fools. I escaped the first time they stopped at a traffic light."

"Seems like they should have been armed."

Rader shrugged his shoulders. "Like I said. Clumsy fools."

Mr. Biggs nodded to the other two men. "Who are they?"

"Uh, undercover agents. They've been with us for years."

"That's odd. I've never met them."

"Yes, well, they probably never came into the office while you were on duty," Rader said, as the two men standing behind him waited to see how this unexpected development would play out.

What was going on here? Lancelot thought. They exchanged conversation as if this were a Saturday-night barbecue. Mr. Rader prided himself in thinking fast. He was a former agent. But he vastly underestimated Mr. Biggs. Perhaps he didn't realize Mr. Biggs was a retired army intelligence officer.

Suddenly, Ted Rader stepped forward with his hand outstretched. "Better give me that thing, Biggs." The fourteen-year-old decoder watched in gut-wrenching horror as Mr. Biggs easily relinquished the gun. He didn't so much as argue about it! Just handed over his last line of defense to the traitor and the foreign agents who were with him.

"No problem," Mr. Biggs said, handing over the gun. He walked directly to a table and picked up a stack of papers Lancelot had studied minutes before. "Wonder how these got here?" he said casually.

"I gave it a quick look. Nothing much there," Rader said. "We're taking everything back to the agency to evaluate the level of damage. We've got everything under control. You may as well clear out."

Mr. Biggs continued leafing through the papers. "'Looks like recently

29

decoded messages," he said, noting the date at the top of the pages.

Lancelot anxiously tried to imagine Mr. Biggs' next maneuver but failed.

"Sorry, Biggs," Rader said, stepping forward. "Didn't want you to get involved. We'll be done in ten minutes, so you just sit in that chair, stay quiet, and nothing will happen to you."

'Nothing will happen to you'? What did that mean? Lancelot's terror-filled gaze rested on Mr. Biggs expecting to see his own reaction mirrored in the man's face. Instead, the head of security folded his arms and sat calmly in the chair situated next to a wall.

Lancelot's eyes shifted rapidly back and forth between the head of security, the traitor, and the two foreign agents. Weren't they here to stop these guys? So how were they going to do that with no gun, Mr. Biggs confined to a chair, and Lancelot cringing behind a door?

Mr. Biggs rotated his shoulders and at the same time slipped his fingers to the inside pocket of his jacket. When he settled back in his chair again, his arms assumed the same crossed position as before. He'd done something, but Lancelot hadn't a clue what it was.

In shifting his glasses, Lancelot accidentally clicked them against the door. It wouldn't have mattered, because of the shattering noise the three men were making. However, at that very second, activity had come to a momentary pause. And they heard him. Mr. Biggs tried to cover with a series of coughs, but the men weren't fooled.

Ted Rader picked up the gun and looked behind the door where Lancelot stood pressed against the wall. His gaze and his gun dropped as his eyebrows rose. "Who are you?" he demanded.

"He's…" Mr. Biggs said.

"You stay out of it! Who are you?"

"I'm, uh, a part-time decoder," Lancelot squeaked.

Rader's eyes screwed nearly shut. "A what?!"

"Part-time decoder."

"Working for the agency?!"

"Well—yes."

Rader moved in closer. "I remember you," he said. "I saw you this week when you dropped off decoded messages into my inbox. What are you doing here?"

"D--doing here?" Lancelot stammered. "Well, uh, actually—I have no idea. But I'm out past curfew, so I think I'd better leave now."

Rader towered menacingly over the boy. "Don't get smart with me, kid." The night-duty officer studied this insignificant interference. "I'll deal with you later," he said in a deep, quiet voice, then shoved him behind the door again. The packing was nearly completed, so he opened a small suitcase, pulled out bundles of hundred-dollar bills and began to count.

For the first time in his entire life, Lancelot was glad he was small for his age. A small build and glasses added to the image of being insignificant, so for the first time in his entire life, he was glad about that, too. If he stayed behind the door, he'd probably be all right. They might forget he was there. Actually, they may have already forgotten about him. And, eventually, the three men would leave. They wouldn't hurt Mr. Biggs. He hoped. Yet, this uncontrollable, inconvenient feeling persisted in rising to the top. He vanquished it from his mind, but it would not be tamped down. Ultimately, it overwhelmed him. He'd played the fourteen-year-old, helpless decoder long enough. The fact that the three men considered him totally nonthreatening was a distinct asset.

Lancelot squared his shoulders, stepped around the protection of the door, and meandered over to the table. He innocently leafed through the remaining papers stacked on the table. "Oh. You hacked into the Practice Manual. That's interesting. Why'd you do that?"

One of the hulking foreign agents scowled at Lancelot, which nearly put the boy off his game. "What do you mean 'Practice Manual'?" he sneered.

Lancelot fumbled with his glasses, nearly knocking them off his face. "Well, uh, it's the manual the agency gives to beginning decoders so they can practice decoding messages. I spent about two weeks on the practice manual, then they gave me real incoming messages to decode," Lancelot said, hesitated a few seconds, then added weakly, "That's all."

Now, all three men used the force of their combined scowls to drive Lancelot behind the door again. There he hid for about twenty seconds while intense whispers volleyed back and forth.

The door whipped open and Rader yanked Lancelot out to the middle of the floor. "Look, kid. I don't know what your game is, but this stuff is not from the practice manual."

"Oh. Okay," Lancelot said, staring at the floor. When Rader loosened his grip, Lancelot prepared to return to his nest.

A great deal of money was on the line for the two foreign agents, and Lancelot suddenly found himself surrounded by all three men heatedly debating across the top of his head whether this kid knew the difference between practice manual material and the real stuff. As their voices rose, the circle tightened until one of the creeps squatted down, grabbed the front of Lancelot's shirt, and drew him nose to nose.

"We can do this the easy way or we can do this the hard way," he said, through bared teeth. "Which is it going to be?"

Lancelot's glasses had slipped off his nose, but he caught them as they shot halfway down his chest. "E-easy way," he said. "For sure."

"Okay. Is that stuff on the table the real deal or is it from the practice manual?"

Lancelot swallowed hard. "Well, uh, which do you want it to be?"

"Just tell me!"

"Oh. Right. Well, it's definitely real."

Rader stepped back, gloating. "What did I tell you?"

The two men exchanged hard looks, then foreign agent number two placed his hands on his knees and stared at Lancelot six inches from his nose. "So, it's definitely genuine."

"Oh!" Lancelot's eyes shifted back and forth between the two men. "Is that what I said? Well, then I guess they are. If that's what I said."

"He's lying because he's scared," the second foreign agent said.

The men collected all the money stacked on the desk, giving Ted Rader hard looks with each stack they shoved back into the suitcase. They locked it and moved rapidly to the door leading to the reception room while Rader gave the best pitch of his life trying to convince the men that everything they saw was authentic and they shouldn't listen to a kid who didn't know anything. The foreign agents gave him a long, cringe-worthy look and walked out, suitcase in hand.

Rader trailed after them, wailing that they couldn't possibly take the word of a kid over his. After twenty years as a trustworthy agent, he knew the difference between practice codes and classified material that had come into the agency.

When Lancelot's knees began to buckle, Mr. Biggs caught him before he hit the floor and ushered him to the chair he'd just vacated. "Good work, kid!"

"It was?" Lancelot said weakly. "But they're getting away."

"The A-Team is waiting outside to grab them."

Lancelot's puzzled face looked up. "A-Team?"

"Half a dozen retired army buddies of mine. They'll take care of it.."

As if on cue, six elderly men shuffled through the door wearing dark clothes and army boots identical to the boots worn by the head of security. When they yanked off their dark knitted hats, three senior citizens had white hair that stood at right angles to their heads; the fourth had no hair at all, which was a sharp contrast to their blackened faces. One of the men leaned slightly on a cane and another fiddled with his hearing aid as they made their way to the far side of the room, where Mr. Biggs joined them.

This was the A-Team?! The "A" must stand for "Ancient". Lancelot studied the men. One of them actually looked old enough to be Mr. Biggs' father. Maybe he was! In any case, what were they doing here dressed for a covert operation? As hard as his ears strained, he heard nothing of the next few minutes' conversation. They were filled with hushed voices, occasional nodding of heads then shaking of heads at other times. Finally, they broke up and Mr. Biggs returned to Lancelot, signaling it was time to leave.

On the way through the reception room, one of the men dropped his cane. Lancelot surged forward to pick it up. "Here you are. I don't want you to fall."

"What?! Fall?!" the senior snarled, glared, then snatched it out of Lancelot's hand. "I can walk just fine without it, sonny!"

Lancelot mumbled something to the effect that he was sorry. He hadn't meant—anything really. He wiped his hands on his t-shirt, then waited until he was sure the oldsters and gangsters had cleared out before venturing outside. It was deathly quiet, which worried him a little. On one hand, he was relieved everyone was gone, but they'd left so quickly. And where were they? No cars, no people, just Mr. Biggs. He turned to the head of security for answers, but all he said was, "Let's go, kid."

"How are we getting back?" Lancelot said.

"Truck."

"It died!"

"No. Just needed a rest."

True to his prophecy, the truck's engine turned over and they rattled and coughed down the street towards Lancelot's house. He drew the gun out of his pocket and tossed it on the seat with the barrel facing Lancelot.

"That thing might go off!"

"Not loaded."

"Not loaded?! Why did you bring it then?"

"Visuals, kid. Good for visuals. Loaded guns are dangerous. I only load it if I absolutely have to. Use strategy and stealth instead."

Lancelot considered that for a moment, eventually turning in his seat to study the head of security, who was quietly humming and tapping out a tune that was popular forty years ago. He was so relaxed for someone who faced down a traitor and two foreign agents. "Who were those men you talked to at the end?"

"Old army buddies."

"Rader and those foreign agents are huge and your army buddies are sort of smallish and a bit sunken. Didn't any of your army buddies get hurt?"

"No. They tackled, disarmed and cuffed all three as they walked out the door."

Lancelot's brows shot up. "Tackled and cuffed? How did they do that?!"

"Leverage and the element of surprise, kid. Lots of leverage."

"What kind of leverage?"

"Stuff we learned in the army. Judo, jiu jitsu, stuff like that."

Lancelot waited, his eyes growing larger the longer he waited. "You mean you were part of the, uh, special stuff the army does?"

"Something like that."

Lancelot knew he'd never get the story beyond "something like that". "The note you took out of Mr. Fillmore's car. What did it say?"

"Confirmed that Rader was the traitor," Mr. Biggs said, scowling deeply. "My one army buddy retired from the agency a few years ago. I called him to arrange backup before I called you. He got there ahead of

Rader. He saw the two foreign agents capture Fillmore and shove him in one of their rented cars. They drove a couple of blocks and left him where we found him then went back to the warehouse. When my buddy saw Rader arrive, he knew he was the traitor. He wrote the note and left it hidden in the car where we found Fillmore."

"But how did your buddy know we'd find the note?"

Mr. Biggs smiled. "He knew I'd see the car and make a search." Before Lancelot could ask, he added. "My buddy hid the note in case one of the foreign agents came back and saw it."

"He knew you'd stop to check the car and make a search," Lancelot said softly. "You and your buddies must know each other very well."

Mr. Biggs hesitated for a moment then said, "We do."

"Why did he leave the note instead of calling you?"

"Rader had already reset the agents' phones to voicemail. He didn't want to take the chance that he'd do the same thing to mine."

Lancelot nodded. They were way ahead of him on anticipating what might happen. "Did you suspect Rader?"

"Not until tonight," Mr. Biggs said. "Two things. All the agents I called had the same voice message using the same voice. And the voice messages were all reset tonight by someone who discovered his cover had just been blown. Another thing. When Rader got ready to leave the agency, he wanted to go out the front door." He glanced at Lancelot. "His car is parked out back."

Lancelot drew his brows together. "If you knew all your army buddies were coming, why did you call me?"

"Figured at some point, we'd have to confront Rader and the

foreign agents. Wanted to give the boys time to get in place outside. Needed to stall Rader and whoever was with him till they got there. Thought you'd be a distraction for them. And you were," Mr. Biggs said. "Anyway, it was a good experience for you. Broadening."

"Good experience?" Lancelot said. "Broadening?"

"You put serious doubts in their minds, so they left the building, which meant my buddies didn't need to risk coming into a potentially dangerous situation. Element of surprise was on our side." When Lancelot was silent, Mr. Biggs added, "You succeeded, didn't you? Did a good job. Great confidence builder."

As they approached his house, Lancelot sat up just a little straighter. His jagged nerves relaxed just a tad to be replaced by the tiniest shred of pride, something he'd never felt before.

The Intruder

The intelligence agency was eerily quiet when Mr. Biggs admitted Lancelot through the front door at nine o'clock on a Saturday morning. Normally, he came to work at three-thirty Monday, Wednesday, and Friday.

His older brother had a big soccer game after school the day before and his mother thought he should attend since his brother was captain of the team and a star player. Afterall, it was his last year in high school and his last game until he left for college where he had a full scholarship because he was a soccer star. Lancelot could have argued the point that his brother didn't really care whether he was there or not but, to please his mother, he attended his brother's game without making a face or a fuss.

"You're working Saturday instead of Friday after school," Mr. Biggs commented.

Lancelot followed Mr. Biggs into his office and leaned against the door. "Yes, I had to go to my brother's soccer game. Both my brothers are big soccer players," he said with a certain amount of envy in his voice.

Mr. Biggs studied the young decoder who was tapping his fingertips on the desk while staring rather morosely at the floor. "Everybody is good at something. You're good at decoding; they're good at soccer," he said. "You'll have a great future in technology someday if that's what you want."

"Do you really think so," Lancelot said, his fingertips stopped tapping as he focused his attention on the head of security.

"Wouldn't say it if I didn't think so, kid."

Lancelot smiled. That was one thing about Mr. Biggs. He never said anything he didn't mean. "Thanks," he said softly.

Hating the limelight for any reason, Mr. Biggs shrugged his shoulders and shuffled a few papers on his desk.

Uplifted by Mr. Biggs' praise, Lancelot left to walk down the hall to the decoding room. Something was different. He stopped in the hallway and listened. He'd never worked on a Saturday morning before and decided what was different was the usual hum of activity that met him during the week was missing. Instead of the buzz of activity, he was met with silence. "Where is everyone?"

"It's Saturday, so most of the regular staff isn't here. Some of the others who normally come in on the weekend are in different places or will be here this afternoon. Just you and me here till about one o'clock, kid," Mr. Biggs said.

Lancelot walked back to Mr. Biggs' doorway. "Where did everybody go?"

"Some are at a conference. Three flew out an hour ago for an emergency mission. Two people from the lab called in sick. Strep throat." Mr. Biggs glanced at Lancelot with a look that said he hoped no one else caught it.

Lancelot nodded in agreement. "Okay, well, I'll just mosey down to the decoding room to see what there is to do." He walked two doors down then sat at his desk and sighed as he looked at the large stack of messages that needed decoding. Obviously the decoder who worked the night shift on Friday hadn't shown up for work either. He settled in for a peaceful three hours of work. After dealing with the noise generated by a soccer game, he needed quiet.

"Leaving my office to make rounds, kid," Mr. Biggs called out from the hallway. "Be back in fifteen minutes." The sound of the elevator door opened and closed followed by the hum of it rising to the floors above.

"Right," Lancelot said. Mr. Biggs didn't usually mention he was leaving his office. Perhaps it was because it was Saturday morning and only the two of them were here. Or, maybe it was a subtle hint to listen for the phone in the security office and answer it if anyone called.

But he wasn't gone for fifteen minutes. Lancelot was decoding a particularly difficult message and lost track of time. When the message was finally decoded and placed in the outbox, he leaned back in his chair and stretched his tense muscles. It was then his eyes glanced at his watch. Thirty minutes had gone by. Where was Mr. Biggs? Had something happened to him? Should he search through the building

41

for him? He felt a sense of relief when he heard the elevator door slide open and footsteps head down the hallway in his direction. Before Lancelot could ask if something had happened, Mr. Biggs stood in his doorway.

"Don't suppose this yours?" the head of security said, holding a boot-sized box wrapped in brown paper.

"No. Never saw it," Lancelot said. "Where was it?"

With great care, Mr. Biggs set it on a nearby table. "Leaning against a door on the top floor."

"Have you ever found anything like this before?"

"No, the staff knows better than to leave something like this," Mr. Biggs said. "This is one of the reasons I make rounds."

"Do you normally make rounds?"

"Make them every two hours. People come and go around here. I want to make sure they lock their doors before they leave."

By now, Lancelot knew Mr. Biggs was a great deal more than the head of security. Everyone in the entire building seemed to defer to him, including Chief. Staff members showed up in his office and conducted lengthy discussions with him behind closed doors.

"The problem is the package wasn't there the last time I made rounds," Mr. Biggs said.

"You mentioned that some people left an hour ago to catch a flight. Could it have been one of them?"

"Might be," Mr. Biggs said, then thought a moment. "But not likely."

"Why do you say that?"

"Like I said, nobody at an intelligence agency would leave a plain-wrapped box like this just lying around somewhere."

"No," Lancelot said softly. "I suppose not."

It wasn't like Mr. Biggs to stop by his office for a casual chat. "Are you worried?"

Mr. Biggs screwed up his mouth for a few seconds. "Yes."

Lancelot put down his pencil and joined Mr. Biggs inside his worry circle. "Why are you worried?"

"When the group left to catch the flight, somebody would have told me about it," Mr. Biggs said, his face reflecting the puzzle of his discovery. "They checked in with me before they left. One of them would have said something about a box left leaning against the door. In fact, they would have left the box with me to avoid confusion."

"But nobody in the staff left the box leaning against a door, so that means…." Lancelot opened his mouth, closed it then tried again. "That means somebody else is in the building," he said, keeping his voice remarkably steady. "How did they get in? There's no way to get in here."

Mr. Biggs nodded his approval. The kid figured it out without having to be told. "That's why I'm worried."

Lancelot quickly reviewed what he knew about the building. "There aren't any windows on the ground floor. They'd have to use a ladder to climb through windows on the other floors." Lancelot felt a sudden dampness where his back rested against the chair. "And the front and back doors are electronically bolted." He didn't like the tone of urgency that had crept into his voice. Then he added the obvious. "If you don't enter a code to unbolt the doors, there's no way to get in here."

"No way to get in," Mr. Biggs said. "No way to get out either unless you know the code." He stroked his chin as he stared at the floor. "No ground-floor windows. Two bolted doors," he murmured, confirming what Lancelot just said. "There's no other way to get in that we know about. So, somebody was clever enough to find another way inside this building, and we need to discover how they did it." Having decided what to do, he pushed away from the door, carefully picked up the box, and walked with purpose down the hall to his office.

Lancelot was hard on his heels. "Has the box got something in it?" he called ahead.

"Box has got something in it, all right," Mr. Biggs said. "Fairly heavy, too. Need to find out what it is and if it's dangerous."

"What are you going to do?" Lancelot said, hovering inside Mr. Biggs' doorway.

Mr. Biggs placed the box on a side table then picked up his phone. After pressing a number, he focused his attention on the box. "Bake? Biggs here. Found a box on the top floor that wasn't there the last time I made rounds." He listened, then said, "No idea. Can the boys come and deal with it?" More listening. "Right, thanks."

"Why did you call Mr. Baker?" Lancelot said.

"Bomb squad," Mr. Biggs said as if he were talking about what he ate for dinner the previous night. "Be here in five minutes."

Lancelot dropped onto the only other chair in the room and stared vacantly, yet somehow anxiously, at the box. "Bomb squad, I didn't know Mr. Baker worked for a bomb squad," he murmured.

"He doesn't. But he knows people who do. Chief calls Bake whenever we have this kind of problem. The team shows up faster if we call Bake first."

Lancelot looked up sharply. "How often do you have this kind of problem?"

Mr. Biggs stared at the floor while his mind worked back over the ten years since he retired from army intelligence and joined the intelligence agency. "This makes the third time."

"So it's happened two other times and this makes the third time," Lancelot said. "Was there ever a real bomb and did it ever explode?"

Mr. Biggs hesitated not wanting to frighten the kid but figured he'd find out sooner or later anyway. "Yes and yes."

"It was a real bomb both times and it actually exploded?!"

"Didn't want to lie to you, kid," Mr. Biggs said. "Nobody got hurt and we found the perpetrators."

"You found the people who planted the bomb here. Who were they?"

"Doesn't matter. They're all in prison now."

"Okay, so we know it couldn't be them," Lancelot said then after thinking this through a few seconds, he said, "Do you think we should, uh, move to another part of the building until Mr. Baker gets here? I mean since we don't know what's inside it."

"Bake will be here in a couple of minutes and I need to be nearby to let him in. In any case, nothing's ticking and nothing happened when I moved it, so I think we'll be all right, for now," Mr. Biggs said, then added, "Better to be safe than sorry. That's why I called Bake. He'll take it away, have a look, then we'll know what we've got."

Lancelot couldn't decide whether to stay with Mr. Biggs in the event he needed emotional support or return to his room and close the door tightly just in case things didn't turn out too well. But Mr. Biggs sat at his desk continuing with the work he'd been doing before he left to make the rounds of the building. Glancing at the head of security he could easily see that emotional support was not needed. In fact, he was the one who needed a little emotional support. So Lancelot continued to sit in his chair and study the box willing it not to explode. Afterall, he had to live long enough to be the hotshot tech person that Mr. Biggs predicted.

In five minutes, the buzzer sounded. Mr. Biggs entered the code that unlocked it.

Mr. Baker and three men burst through. The three men wore thickly padded uniforms that covered their entire bodies including their heads.

"In there, Bake," Mr. Biggs said, pointing to his office.

Mr. Baker stood in the hallway while the other men walked rapidly into the security office, then closed the door firmly behind them. He glanced at Lancelot then said, "Why don't you take the kid out back, Biggs? We'll put the box in a bomb-proof container and take it away. Be out of here in a few minutes. I'll holler when we're done."

"Good idea," Mr. Biggs said, then turned to Lancelot. "Let's go, kid."

Lancelot energetically led the way down the hall to the backdoor then stepped aside while Mr. Biggs spent an eternity entering the code. When they were finally outside, he walked to the old, misshapen, rusted-out heap Mr. Biggs referred to as his truck. If not necessarily reliable, at least it was familiar. He'd been an unwilling passenger in it several times, so it was a little like going home. "Have you called the bomb squad before?"

"No. First time. The other two times, we didn't know about the bomb until it exploded."

"How could you not know there was a bomb in the building?" Lancelot said. "There's a sensor at the door that detects things like that."

"They didn't bring the bomb in fully assembled and ready to go off otherwise it would have set off an alarm. They brought it in over a period of a week, assembled it, and that's when it went off. They thought it would bring down the building and everyone in it. Fortunately, they miscalculated badly and no one got hurt. Not much damage to the building either," Mr. Biggs said then looked at the decoder. "So we're lucky this time."

Lancelot wasn't sure he felt lucky but at least they were still alive. "I've seen Mr. Baker several times now. The two of you were in the army together, right? You called him because he's a friend of yours and you knew he'd call the right people."

"Yes, he's an old army buddy of mine."

"That's why you didn't have to give him your address," Lancelot said.

"Right. Bake's been here before," Mr. Biggs said.

"Do you have a lot of army buddies?"

"Spent thirty years in the army. I've got lots of them."

The backdoor opened and Mr. Baker gave them the all-clear signal. He waited until they reached him and they walked down the hall together. "They've taken it to a lab. Given it top priority. Don't know what they'll find, Biggs. I'll give you a call when I find out."

"Thanks, Bake. Not sure what we're dealing with here. That box showed up out of nowhere," Mr. Biggs said.

After he left, Mr. Biggs closed the front door and reset the electronic code. He unlocked his desk and slowly took out a key card, then looked at Lancelot. "Master key card. Opens every door in the building. Need to see if anything's out of place."

"But I thought you already checked the building when you made rounds."

"Didn't go inside the rooms. Just checked to see if the doors were locked."

"Every room in the building?"

"Every room."

"Even Chief's office on the fourth floor?" Lancelot whispered.

"Especially Chief's office. Box was leaning against his door."

Lancelot's mouth dropped open as he stared at Mr. Biggs. "The box was leaning against Chief's door?"

Mr. Biggs nodded as he glanced at Lancelot. "That's one of the reasons I'm worried."

"Do you think they intended to, well, hurt the Chief?"

"Don't know yet. Don't know if the person who planted it there knew it was Chief's office. Probably did, but no proof yet."

"Does Chief know that yet?" Lancelot said.

"Not yet," Mr. Biggs said. "He'll want questions answered, and I don't have any answers to give him right now. Anyway, he's out of town at a conference. Don't want to alert him until I'm sure I need to."

Lancelot continued to hover as Mr. Biggs locked his middle desk drawer, then unlocked a metal cabinet to the side of the desk. "Are you taking anything to, uh, protect yourself in case the other guy brought something to protect himself?"

Mr. Biggs folded his arms with lips pressed into a straight line as he stared into the cabinet. He shut the cabinet door then headed down the hallway to the basement with Lancelot close behind. He traveled the length of the room and stopped in front of a shelf Lancelot remembered from before.

"This is where you got the detector to check for a listening device in your office.

"Yes, this is where I got it," Mr. Biggs said, glancing at the boy who remembered everything for better or worse. He placed the detector inside his pocket and returned to the main floor where he stood in front of the elevator.

"Uh, want me to make the rounds with you?" Lancelot waited, but Mr. Biggs didn't respond. Was it because he didn't hear him or didn't want to discuss it? Lancelot decided to repeat the question. "Want me to go with you?"

"No."

Lancelot's ears were disconnected from his brain, so he trailed after Mr. Biggs to the elevator. When the doors opened, he slipped in behind the older man. When Mr. Biggs turned around his eyebrows shot up. Desperation is the mother of creativity. "I wouldn't want you to face whatever is out there by yourself," he said, rather lamely.

Mr. Biggs' eyes twinkled briefly, he nodded, then pressed number "2" on the panel.

As the elevator rose to the second floor, Lancelot said, "Do you think we should call a backup team to help search the building?"

"Only if I need to. Reconnaissance trip first. See what's up there."

"I know, but what if we find a gang of violent people or something like that?"

Mr. Biggs glanced at Lancelot then back to the panel. "Not usually 'a gang of people' for something like this."

"Oh," Lancelot said. As the elevator door opened, he debated whether he should stay out of the way and wait in the decoding room. In the end, he followed behind Mr. Biggs to the end of the hallway, stood to the side as Mr. Biggs inserted the key card, and shoved the door open.

Mr. Biggs flipped on the light, then waited and listened before stepping into the room. First, his eyes traveled around the office, studying the ceiling, floor, furniture, and trash cans. When nothing appeared to be out of order, he walked around the room with the detector checking for a listening device but the light within the detector didn't blink.

"What are you looking for?" Lancelot said from the safety of the doorway.

"Anything unlocked or been obviously tampered with. We're probably dealing with a professional rather than an amateur so I doubt if I find anything tampered with," Mr. Biggs said. "But it's better to be thorough rather than wish you had been."

"How can you tell if somebody's tampered with it?"

"Uh," Mr. Biggs said absently. "Might be a slight dent in a cabinet where somebody tried to force it open. Maybe a scratch beside the lock where he used a tool to try to open it. Might be a small bug somewhere which is why I brought the listening detector. Papers left out, which is against regulations. Doubt if I find any of those things. That would indicate a very clumsy amateur. Any professional hacker can find out what's on the computer from the outside, so I don't worry about checking that. In any case, it's very difficult to break through our antivirus protection systems." He stepped over to the window, searching every inch, then turned away.

"Did you find anything?"

"No," Mr. Biggs said. He locked the door and went to the office next door, repeating the process.

As they came out of the room, Mr. Biggs' phone rang. "Bake, find anything?" His brow tightened as he listened to the test results. "It was an explosive but no detonator so no chance it could have exploded. Okay, thanks, Bake."

"Nothing dangerous? That's good."

"Right. Bake said they x-rayed it. It's an explosive but the detonator is missing."

Lancelot didn't know how to respond, so he said nothing as he followed Mr. Biggs into the third room. He provided a set of inexperienced, nervous eyes as the search continued. Having checked every office on the second floor, they returned to the elevator.

Mr. Biggs' lips were inside his mouth while he stared hard at the elevator floor. When they reached the third floor, they exited together and rounded the corner, then pulled up short. There, leaning against the last door in the hallway, was a brown, paper-covered box identical to the one found on the fourth floor earlier that morning.

"Wait here," Mr. Biggs ordered.

Maybe Mr. Biggs didn't need Lancelot's moral support after all. He could always slip down the stairway exit and wait in the decoding room.

Except they hadn't checked the stairway yet. Who knew what lurked within that cavernous, echoing silo? And there was another reason. He'd offered to help and didn't want to back out when the going got tougher.

Mr. Biggs eyed the box for a few seconds, lifted it an inch off the floor, and put it down a foot to the side so they could enter the room.

At the opposite end of the hallway, Lancelot wondered why he did that. Why didn't he take it to his office, call Mr. Baker, and ask him to pick it up?

Mr. Biggs took out his phone. "Bake? Biggs here. Found another box." He listened for a few seconds. "Same size. Same everything except this one is slightly heavier. The problem is, we don't know if the extra weight is because it has a detonator." A longer silence this time. "No idea what's going on. Calling Chief as soon as I finish my rounds. Maybe sooner. I'm searching the rest of the building right now. I'll wait until I'm finished to call you. No use coming to pick up this one if there are more."

When Lancelot got the go-ahead signal, he trotted purposefully down the hallway. "What did Mr. Baker say?"

"He agreed it's better to wait until we're done with the building in case there are more boxes." Mr. Biggs unlocked the door, stepped through, and followed the same routine he'd used with all the other offices.

Lancelot stood hesitantly in the doorway, staring at the maybe dangerous, maybe innocent box. "Somebody wanted us to think it might explode. Why go to all that trouble and not attach a detonator to it?"

"Didn't want the place to blow up," Mr. Biggs said. "They're trying to focus our time and attention away from the goal?"

"What do you think the goal is?"

"No idea."

Lancelot absently ruffled his hair, then pushed up his glasses. "How did he get in here in the first place?" he said, then added more quietly, "Where is he now? And can he hear or see us?"

"Don't know. Yet."

As the elevator rose to the fourth floor, the head of security frowned pensively as he thought of the second box they'd just discovered.

"Why didn't we find a box on the second floor?" Lancelot said.

"Working his way down the building."

Sometimes, Lancelot had difficulty deciphering what Mr. Biggs said, but this time, his meaning was crystal clear. "You mean. Do you mean…."

"Yes. He's been to the fourth and third floors. Just hasn't gotten to the second floor yet."

"Do you think he will?"

"Sooner or later."

"Why haven't we run into him yet? It's so quiet, we can hear the tiniest squeak. Anyway, why would a man want to sneak in here this time of day?"

"Don't know if the intruder's a man yet."

"But you've been saying 'he' all along," Lancelot said.

"Turn of phrase. That's all."

"So it might be a girl— a woman? Why do you think that?"

53

"Size."

"What's size got to do with it?"

Mr. Biggs stared at the ceiling of the elevator. "Probably found a way to get in through the roof then the ventilation shaft. Have to be small to do that. Could be a small man or a small woman. Wait and see."

"But why is he doing this?"

"Got an idea. Just not sure of it yet."

Lancelot waited, then finally said with more exasperation than he intended, "Well, what's your idea?"

Mr. Biggs looked down at Lancelot. "Later."

They exited the elevator on the fourth floor with caution. Mr. Biggs peered around the corner of the elevator then, with Lancelot dogging his tracks, walked to the end of the hallway where he found the first box. Mr. Biggs unlocked Chief's office and stepped inside. He inspected the room glancing steadily at the listening device detector in case it started to blink. His eyes traveled the perimeter of the room finally coming to rest on the huge grate covering the ventilation shaft. He studied every inch of its four edges, allowing his fingertips to follow his focus.

Lancelot peered over his shoulder. When Mr. Biggs' fingertips suddenly stopped, he said, "What do you see?"

Mr. Biggs tapped a spot on the wall right beside the grate. "Right there," he said, suddenly whispering. "The grate doesn't quite line up."

Mr. Biggs never whispered. Lancelot studied him nervously as the head of security drew his finger to his lips. "Line up with what?" he said, his voice barely audible.

Mr. Biggs drew Lancelot closer to the wall. "See that thin line? That line is a little darker than the rest of the paint on the wall. All the rooms are painted white, but over time sunlight fades paint. Even white fades. Where the grate touches the wall, the paint is a little brighter, like the original color. Somebody's moved this grate. Recently, too."

With trembling fingers, Lancelot pushed his glasses farther up on his nose. "So he came into Chief's office through this hole?"

"More than likely. More than likely left that way, too."

Lancelot stared at Mr. Biggs. "Aren't the grates screwed into the wall? How could somebody unscrew them from the inside?"

"He planned ahead and brought the right tools."

Lancelot tried to visualize how that could be done and failed. But he didn't fail to visualize something even more terrifying. "That's how he's going through the building. Pushes out the ventilation grates, gets inside the rooms, and does whatever he's here to do, then leaves the room through the same hole."

"Right. The grate was lined up perfectly with the paint on the third floor so I couldn't see that it had been moved."

It wasn't much of a stretch to visualize pushing the grate out of the wall or climbing back into the ventilation shaft. "I don't see how anyone could climb back into that hole carrying the heavy grate, then put it into place."

Mr. Biggs inserted his fingers through the holes in the grate and eased it quietly off the wall. "Most people couldn't. But he's a professional."

A professional what? But Mr. Biggs' attention moved in another direction before he could ask.

Mr. Biggs focused his flashlight down the length of the shaft, then motioned for Lancelot to look.

"What am I supposed to see?"

"Shafts get dusty," Mr. Biggs whispered. "See the line in the dust heading down the shaft? Sometimes the line gets wider, then narrows down."

Stepping forward, Lancelot stared down the long, square, ventilation shaft. The hole was huge compared to what he'd imagined it would be. No telling how far it went. "I see it. Is that line in the dust important?"

"The line is where he dragged his body through the dust. The line gets wider because he tied the boxes he brought along to his ankle and dragged them behind him. Sometimes the boxes are right behind his body; sometimes they slipped to the side."

"He was up here the whole time." Lancelot looked at Mr. Biggs. "And we didn't know anything about it."

"Like I said, he's a professional." Mr. Biggs eyes narrowed. "With professionals, it's always like that."

Lancelot's focus returned to the enormous hole in the wall. The metal pathway narrowed into utter darkness. And the intruder used this to navigate his way through the building. "None of the rooms are that big in this building. Why is the ventilation-shaft hole so huge?"

"Used to be a warehouse. Agency bought it and divided it into office space." Mr. Biggs hesitated as he folded his arms and stared at Lancelot, "Look, kid. I've got an idea. I think it will work, but I need your help."

"Me? How can I be of any help? Shouldn't you call somebody else for help?"

"Yes. Plan to call them on my way to the basement."

"Can't we wait until they get here to work on your idea?" Lancelot said evasively.

Biggs pressed his lips inward, then said, "Intruder could be long gone by then. Got to do something now or he may escape then we'll never know who he is or what he's doing here."

Lancelot leaned against the wall and waited as his face turned the same shade as the wall. "Okay. What do you want me to do?"

"Tell you when I get back. Right now, I need to make a trip to the basement where the blueprints of the building are stored. While I'm there, I'll pick up the tools we'll need. You wait here."

"Couldn't I come with you?"

"Blueprints are locked up and classified. Be back in a couple of minutes."

Lancelot stared incredulously at Mr. Biggs, then at the grate. "Couldn't we put that thing back while you're gone?" he said, forgetting to whisper.

Mr. Biggs' finger rose to his lips again. "Taking out the grate was one thing, but I'd have to pound around the edges to get it in place."

"But the intruder got it into place," Lancelot argued.

Mr. Biggs raised an eyebrow. "Just barely. Hung by a thread. Could have fallen out when somebody slammed the door shut. Don't want to run the risk of it crashing to the floor."

Lancelot sighed. "He'd hear it and know we were onto him."

Mr. Biggs headed for the door, then stopped. "Look, kid. When I get back, you're going to have to put on your brave boots."

"Brave boots? What's that mean?" Lancelot said, but Mr. Biggs had already left. He didn't particularly like the sound of "brave boots" or the meaning behind it. He looked at the grate then the hole. What if the intruder came back? He stepped outside the room into the hallway and walked rapidly to the end, then turned around and walked back. He repeated this until he heard the sound of the elevator. Somewhat out of breath, he returned to the room and struck what he hoped was a manly pose in keeping with his brave-boots image.

Mr. Biggs quietly entered the room with a number of objects. Three looked like adjustable braces. There was a wrench, two towels, a rope and a hardhat that held a miniature flashlight in the front.

"What are you going to do with those?"

"Nothing. You're going to do something with them."

Lancelot's manly pose suffered a setback. "Me? How can I do anything with them? Anyway, how come I'm the one who has to do something with them?"

"Got arthritis. Can't do that kind of thing anymore unless it's an emergency. You have to do it."

"You don't understand," Lancelot said. "I am a decoder. I have no training whatsoever in ventilation-shaft reconnaissance. Anyway, can't we just wait ten more minutes until somebody gets here?"

Mr. Biggs' face hardened. "There's a problem, kid."

Lancelot stared in silence, then whispered, "What kind of problem?"

"He put a jamming device in place. Land phones and cell phones don't work."

Lancelot stared disbelievingly, then stepped to Chief's desk and picked up the land phone. It was dead. Suddenly, a thought occurred to him. "We can leave the building and make a call when we're outside."

"There's another problem." Mr. Biggs pressed his lips into a straight line. "Can't do that either."

"Why can't we do that?"

"Jammed the signal from the panel to the doors."

"What does mean?" Lancelot said although he already knew.

"When I punch in the code to unlock the doors, they don't unlock."

"You mean—you mean we can't get out?"

"We can't get out."

Lancelot returned his stare disbelievingly. "There has to be a way to override what he's done."

"There is. I have to reprogram it. I can do that, but it'll take time," Mr. Biggs said, then added, "Well, I can probably do that. Depends on what he's done."

Lancelot crumbled wordlessly onto a chair, then looked up. "We're trapped," he said, his voice so soft it was barely audible.

"Not trapped. Just inconvenienced for a while. Right now, we've got other things to think about." Mr. Biggs took the boy's arm and drew him to the ventilation shaft in the wall. "Look, kid." When Lancelot's eyes failed to meet his, he shook his arm, bringing him back to focus. "We need to win, so pay attention."

Lancelot nodded. "I understand."

"About fifteen feet into that shaft, you come to a place where you can turn left or right. If you turn left, it leads to the rest of the building. If you turn right, it leads to a ladder which takes you up to the roof of this building," Mr. Biggs said. "Now. I checked the blueprints. I figure he had to come in through the roof, climb down the ladder, and drag himself through the shaft till he got to the first place he could turn. Somehow, he must have gained access to the building's blueprints because he knew Chief's office was at the end of that turn. Once he got into this room, he opened the door and placed the package in front of it. When he finished, he crawled back into the shaft, dragged himself along, and turned left to get to the rest of the building. It's all about freedom of movement."

Lancelot swallowed and straightened his back about halfway. "What do you mean 'freedom of movement'?"

"It's army lingo. Right now, the invader can move all over the building because the ventilation shaft is open. If we block off sections of it, he won't have freedom of movement to go wherever he wants to. We'll control where he can and can't go. The big issue is, he won't be able to escape through the roof. He'll be trapped inside the building. Got that?"

"I got it. We've got to trap him inside this building before he reaches the roof and escapes," Lancelot said. "And fifteen feet down this shaft is the last exit he'll come to when he tries to leave."

"Right." Mr. Biggs placed everything on the floor but the rope, then studied Lancelot's face to see if it would harden to the task. "You ready, kid?"

Lancelot's gaze rose and he nodded. "I'm ready."

"Good man," Mr. Biggs said. "I'll tie this rope around your ankle. Once you block off the shaft, wiggle your foot and I'll pull you back into the room." When Lancelot nodded, he picked up one of the braces and continued, "Remember this. When he left here, he crawled along the shaft until he came to the left turn. You'll fit this brace inside the shaft of that left turn. It should be a fairly tight fit, but you'll need the wrench to turn these bolts until it's so tight, he won't be able to move it and escape through the roof."

"But you said he has tools."

"Couldn't carry a whole box of them," Mr. Biggs said with assurance. "Only brought what he absolutely needed. Anyway, bolts are on your side and they're a lot larger than the ones on the grate. He won't be able to get to them."

As Mr. Biggs knelt and tied the rope, Lancelot mentally wrote his letter of resignation. It was a well-rehearsed letter. He'd written it before, so it didn't take him long to go from "Dear Chief" to "Regrettably, Lancelot Maddox".

Mr. Biggs demonstrated tightening the bolts on the brace. "Now, when you think it's tight enough, give the wrench another quarter turn." He eyed Lancelot as he wrapped the small towel tightly around the wrench, then encased the brace in another towel. "So they don't make any noise," he explained. He slid the brace and wrench as deep into the shaft as he could reach then studied Lancelot.

"Look, kid. The shaft is big enough to crawl through it. If you do that, you'll get to the turn much faster but your knees will make too much noise. Lay flat and pull yourself forward with your forearms. Got that?" When Lancelot nodded, he placed the hardhat on the boy's head and flipped on the tiny flashlight. "Take off your shoes. They'll clunk against the metal." He waited a few more seconds, then gave him a leg-up into the shaft. "Push everything ahead of you until you get to the correct spot," he whispered. "Yank on the rope with your leg when you're finished and I'll pull you back into the room."

The space was even larger than it looked. Lancelot lifted his head and the flashlight lit the way. He pushed the towel-covered brace and wrench ahead then used his forearms to pull himself along. The motions and corresponding sounds were repeated for fifteen feet. The soft material brushed against metal followed by the heavier sound of Lancelot dragging himself through the metal shaft.

Just before the left turn, he stopped. The left turn led to the rest of the building; the right turn led to the roof where the person entered the building. He rested his forehead on his arm, wishing he'd removed his sweater. He peered around the corner, waited, and listened. The only thing he heard was the rapid beat of his heart within his ears.

He unwrapped the brace and shoved it into place then waited. As quietly as he tried to position the brace, had the man heard it somewhere within the ventilation system? When he didn't hear any movement, he edged forward, grabbed the towel which held the wrench, then scooted back. Moving backwards was harder than it looked, which is why Mr. Biggs attached the rope to his ankle.

He hesitated, afraid to unwrap the wrench for fear he'd drop it. Although he didn't hear a sound from Mr. Biggs, somehow, from fifteen feet away, he felt the older man urging him on. He freed the wrench and tightened the bolts, then gave each of them another quarter turn. He tested it and it seemed solidly in place. The job completed, he pulled the wrench and towels to his chest and wiggled his ankle. The return trip was accomplished so quickly Lancelot grabbed his hat before it bounced off the metal and echoed throughout the entire building.

Mr. Biggs caught Lancelot just before the boy crumpled to the floor. He half-carried him to a chair where Lancelot eased his head back against the wall. "Good man," he said softly. He wiped Lancelot's face with a towel, patted his head then looked at his watch. He waited another thirty seconds, then helped him to his feet. "Got two more floors to go, kid."

Lancelot's eyes widened, then he nodded weakly. He trailed along to the elevator, where he mentally prepared himself to enter the shaft right underneath Chief's office.

In the next room, Mr. Biggs gave the anxious decoder another leg-up then placed his hands on the edge of the shaft as he watched Lancelot scoot forward. The kid had spunk and determination.

When Lancelot reached the juncture in the ventilation shaft on the third floor, he again waited and listened. Tentatively, he stretched his neck and peered around the corner, unwrapped the brace, and shoved it into place. He nearly dropped the wrench but grabbed it before it warned the intruder that he was no longer alone in the ventilation shaft. Laying his damp forehead in the crook of his arm, he allowed himself a full ten seconds for a semi meltdown, then another ten seconds to recover. He used both hands to tighten each bolt. With every turn, he glanced down the shaft. As soon as he'd given the last bolt its final quarter turn, he wiggled his ankle and was immediately swept away.

"How'd it go, kid?" Mr. Biggs said as lowered Lancelot onto the chair. Even though Lancelot nodded, Mr. Biggs gave him a little more time to recover. Finally, they moved onto the elevator and down to the second floor.

As he leaned against the elevator wall, Lancelot was still catching his breath. It was only partly because of the physical exertion of dragging himself along the shaft then tightening the brace. Much of it was the mental strain of wondering if he would come face to face with the intruder when he reached the shaft he needed to block. What would he do if that happened? The other person was a trained foreign agent or terrorist. He was only a fourteen-year-old, out-of-shape decoder.

When they rounded the corner on the second floor, they pulled up short. They'd forgotten about the boxes on the third and fourth floors. They were so absorbed in denying the intruder freedom of movement that their entire focus was in trapping him on the first floor. There, leaning against the door they planned to enter, was a box. It was the same shape and size as the others.

Mr. Biggs stroked the side of his face as he readjusted his plan.

"What are you going to do?"

"Not sure. Trying to decide if he put a detonator on this one or some kind of movement sensitive device that explodes if it's' moved. The box on the third floor was heavier than the one on the fourth floor, so he added something to it. He may have added something even more troublesome to this one."

"But why would he put something that senses movement on this one and not the other two."

"He didn't put a detonator on the first box and it was lighter. He may have done that to lull us into thinking that none of them would explode. The second box was heavier so I figure he probably added a detonator.

Lancelot manly pose underwent a serious setback. "I don't want to get blown up today."

"Nobody does, kid."

"What are you going to do?"

"Wait here." Mr. Biggs approached the box slowly, started to move it aside, then changed his mind.

When Mr. Biggs returned, Lancelot said, "Why didn't you move it?"

"Felt heavier than the second box we found."

Lancelot stared at the head of security. "This one is different from the second one. It might have the movement sensor on it like you said."

"Might. Don't know, but it's heavier, which is not a good sign."

Lancelot's eyes drifted to the floor where the heap of equipment lay waiting. "How are we going to block the shaft?"

Mr. Biggs' eyes fidgeted, occasionally coming to rest on him.

The head of security didn't respond and Lancelot didn't want to ask. He was often involved in the bad news and he had already surpassed his quota for bad news in one day. But Lancelot's clever mind sorted through the puzzle. Once he solved it, and all the pieces were in place, he realized the entire success of this mission fell on him.

Mr. Biggs had solved it immediately and was waiting for Lancelot to draw the same conclusion.

"I can get there from the room beside it. I'll just have farther to go."

Mr. Biggs' focus rested on the boy. "I know, but can you do it?"

"I don't know," Lancelot said. "That guy is just waiting for me to pop my head around the corner then he'll bash it in with one of his tools!"

"Unlikely, but it might happen."

Lancelot didn't straighten his shoulders or his face. He just walked down the hall and into the second room from the end.

Mr. Biggs walked directly to the grate and pulled it off the wall. He shone the flashlight down the length of the shaft but couldn't see the end.

About six feet into the shaft, there was a hump that arched over the last office in the hallway. He'd need to crawl over the hump, then pull himself another fifteen feet to the juncture.

"Will the rope reach that far?" Lancelot said.

"No. The rope will be about three feet short of the opening. I'll stand on a chair, lean into the shaft, and get you back just as fast."

Lancelot nodded then shoved the wrapped brace and wrench as far into the shaft as he could while Mr. Biggs tied the rope around his ankle. "What should I do if he's at the juncture waiting for me?"

"If that happens or you hear him coming, wiggle the rope. I'll get you back."

"What if the rope gets caught on something over that hump?" Lancelot said.

"Doesn't pay to think too far ahead, kid," Mr. Biggs said, then gave Lancelot a leg up into the shaft.

The towel-covered items kept falling back as Lancelot tried to push them ahead over the hump. He had the same problem with pulling his body forward. The greater problem was preventing everything from crashing to the bottom once he reached the top. He clasped the items to his chest, held onto his hat, and slid coming to a halt four feet into the straightaway. Now he only had eleven more feet to reach the spot where that section of the ventilation shaft needed to be blocked off.

In a final pull, he reached the edge of the shaft. He tilted his head and looked down the shaft, but it was too dark to see anything. He took off his hat and shone it down the length of the shaft, but saw nothing and, just as importantly, heard nothing. Quickly, he positioned the brace, but it didn't fit as tightly as the others. He reached for the wrench, then stopped.

There it was. A sound identical to the one he made sliding over the hump. He willed his ankle to jerk but it remained still. He needed to escape. Who knew how much time he had before he came face to face with the intruder?

Was it cowardly to run or, in this case, slide to safety? The third and fourth floors were blocked off. At least the intruder would be trapped on the bottom two floors. Then Mr. Biggs' face floated in front of him. He couldn't let him down.

It took both of his unsteady hands to fit the wrench over each bolt. He tightened then tested. Not tight enough. Sweat dripped into his eyes, and he wiped his face with the towel.

The sound changed. It was much louder than before. In his rush to escape, the intruder had lifted himself onto his hands and knees and was now crawling as rapidly as he could to leave the building before he was caught. But had he finished his mission? Was the intruder's mission to position these boxes on each floor, jam the internal phone system and both doors then leave?

Lancelot froze as something occurred to him that he was sure Mr. Biggs and Mr. Baker had already considered. Maybe the explosives had a timing device set to go off at a certain time. If the intruder didn't leave by then, he'd be blown up with everyone and everything else. That was a paralyzing thought. But, if they caught him, the intruder would have to remove the detonator or whatever made the bombs explode in order to save his own life and theirs as well.

Putting all fears aside, Lancelot gave each bolt the final quarter turn, then frantically wiggled his ankle. Grabbing the towels and wrench to his chest, he felt the first tug. Halfway up the hump, with his body hanging downward, everything stopped. He hung suspended with the blood rushing to his head. Finally, he was over the hump and sliding down the shaft to the entrance.

Mr. Biggs caught him and pivoted Lancelot's body onto the chair. "You okay, kid?"

It took Lancelot a few seconds to catch his breath. "I heard something."

"What did it sound like?" Mr. Biggs said, his eyes narrowing.

"Somebody moving. At first, he was dragging himself along like I do. He must have panicked because he started to crawl. He didn't worry about anyone hearing him."

Mr. Biggs stared just above Lancelot's head then returned his focus. "Heading toward you or away from you?"

"I couldn't tell," Lancelot said, and thought a few seconds. "Towards me. He had to be coming in my direction because the sound grew louder."

Mr. Biggs nodded, then replaced the grate over the ventilation shaft. "Come on," he said. But when Lancelot didn't rise from the chair, he placed all the equipment on the floor, pulled him to his feet, pressed him down the hallway, and into the elevator.

"What are we going to do now?"

"Wait," Mr. Biggs said.

"Waiting isn't going to help! We've got to do something!"

"I am."

"Like what?"

"Now that the intruder can't escape, I'm going to reprogram the software so we can open the doors."

Lancelot closed his eyes and laid his head against the elevator wall. "Oh. I forgot about that."

When the elevator reached the ground floor, Mr. Biggs headed straight for his office while Lancelot stumbled after him. The head of security placed his phone and master key card on the desk. "Look, kid. I need quiet while I reprogram this thing. Go to the decoding room and try not to worry about it."

"I don't know if I can do that."

"Try," Mr. Biggs said, then sat at his desk.

Lancelot edged along the wall and into his office, where he closed and locked the door. The intruder was trapped. His freedom of movement was restricted. But he couldn't remain holed up in the ventilation shaft forever. He'd have to leave at some point. What would he and Mr. Biggs do when confronted by him?

He fidgeted over the message he'd started to decode until something subtle broke through. He tilted then turned his head. He carefully laid down his pencil and redirected his attention to the door. The doors were designed to muffle the sound of voices passing through them for

69

security purposes. So the sound was barely audible, but he realized it was a low-level murmur of voices.

Lancelot rose from his chair and silently unlocked the door. He opened it an inch and listened. Even though the voices were lowered, one voice was demanding; the other was angry. He didn't understand what they were saying. He took off his shoes and tiptoed down the hallway, stopping a foot from the door. They were speaking in a language he'd never heard before.

Leaning forward, he saw someone dressed completely in black, covered in dust, with his back to the door facing Mr. Biggs. He couldn't see his hands, but his right elbow was bent. Probably held a gun or knife. He took another step until his line of vision included the head of security.

Mr. Biggs stood with his hands on his hips, glaring at the intruder. He didn't appear frightened but then, Mr. Biggs never appeared frightened. His eyes flicked to his desk then, just as quickly, returned to the demanding voice of the intruder. Was he trying to tell Lancelot something? There it was again, that fraction-of-a-second flicking of the eyes.

He looked at the desk. Mr. Biggs' phone and the master key to all the offices rested on the edge not five feet from where Lancelot stood. But what was he expected to do with them? There was no reception inside the building and he couldn't take the phone outside either. But there it was yet again. The flicking of his eyes. What if he grabbed the phone and master key card then dropped them? What if the floor creaked? Did it creak? He couldn't remember.

Lancelot took a deep breath, reached forward, and grabbed the phone and master key card. Now what? Obviously Mr. Biggs expected him to call for help. That wasn't going to happen unless he could blast a hole through the front door. He closed his eyes for a moment as he realized one of the two boxes might explode before they could escape. Obviously, Mr. Biggs had an idea but what was it?

He tiptoed down the hall to the decoding room and slipped on his shoes. Slowly, it dawned on him that he could get outside. Not easily or pleasantly, but it could be done.

Lancelot walked quickly to the back stairway. He closed his eyes, willing the door not to creak. Miraculously it didn't.

He took the steps two at a time until he reached the second floor. Pressing through the door, he ran to the office they'd just left, grabbed the hat then stopped. What if the intruder had heard him, tied up Mr. Biggs, and was on his way up the backstairs to find him? His eyes fell on the wrench. He picked it up along with the towel and took the stairs two at a time to the fourth floor.

Inside Chief's office, he collapsed onto a chair until his breathing returned to normal or as normal as it was going to get. With the hat placed securely on his head and the towel-covered wrench in his hand, he climbed onto the chair and launched himself into the ventilation shaft. It was pitch black. He fumbled until he found the light switch. If his strategy failed miserably, at least it would be light enough to see its spectacular downfall.

Lancelot shoved the towel-covered wrench in front then pulled himself forward. When he reached the juncture where he'd placed the brace, it looked slightly different. He took off his hat and positioned the light six inches away, following it around the entire perimeter. Yes. There were signs that the intruder had tried to move it and failed. He'd been here then must have moved quickly down to the third floor hoping to get out of the ventilation shaft before they got there. But then, he must have heard them coming and moved down to the second floor.

But what happened after that? How did he escape into the building? The box was in front of the door of the last office in the hallway on the second floor. That's why they used the office next to the end and he was forced to go over the hump. Would the intruder have left the shaft and waited inside the end office? He must have. He must have waited until they left the second floor then came out into the hallway and taken the stairs down to the ground floor where he was arguing with Mr. Biggs this very minute.

Replacing his hat, he twisted his body in the opposite direction and pulled himself down the length of the right shaft leading to the roof. Not knowing how far it was to the end was the worst part. Just when he was sure the blueprints had been wrong, he saw a faint circle of light on the floor just ahead. When he reached the spot, he looked up. The intruder took off the cover leading into the ventilation shaft but hadn't replaced it. Probably for a fast escape. Luck was on Lancelot's side, so far.

Uncovering the wrench, he stuck it through his belt and climbed the ladder. The roof was a large flat area beside other flat-roofed buildings.

Slowly, he turned in a circle, casting his eyes towards the horizon. The breeze blew through his hair as the sun beat down on his face. Freedom never tasted so good.

The weight of the phone in his pocked drew him back. Mr. Baker was the last person called. Lancelot pressed the number and waited.

"Biggs?" Mr. Baker said. "Everything okay?"

"This isn't Mr. Biggs," Lancelot said in a rush.

Mr. Baker hesitated. "Well, who is it?"

"Lancelot Maddox. I was the kid you saw with Mr. Biggs."

"Right, Lancelot. Where's Biggs?"

Lancelot had rehearsed what to say and now it spilled out. "That's why I'm calling. There's an intruder in the building. He got in through the ventilation shaft in the roof, which is where I am right now. He jammed the phones so we can't contact anyone while we're in the building. And he jammed the signal to the doors so we can't get out of the building either. He's trapped Mr. Biggs in his office and I need your help."

"Does he have a gun?"

"I can't tell. His back was to me. His elbow was bent like he might be pointing something at Mr. Biggs."

"What do you need me to do?" Mr. Baker said with a firm voice.

Lancelot was tired of wearing his brave boots. "I don't know?! We just need help!"

"Okay, kid. Do you know anybody who works at the agency that we can call?"

"No! I don't know how to get hold of anyone! Not even Chief!"

"Okay. We'll be there. Wait on the roof so we can see where you are," Mr. Baker said, then added, "Don't leave the roof. Got that?"

"Yes. I'm to wait on the roof so you can see where I am."

73

Lancelot paced around the perimeter of the roof, counting with each lap. By the time he got to thirty, he heard the faint sound of something approaching. It couldn't be, yet it sounded like a helicopter. He shielded his eyes and looked up. Way up. It hovered then moved farther down the row of buildings, slowly descending till it was thirty feet from where he stood.

When it was about two feet above the roof, the helicopter stopped and hovered while four men got out. They were dressed in brown and green camouflage uniforms. Lancelot's eyes widened. They'd sent the army?! Just as quickly, he closed his eyes. It was Mr. Baker and the A-Team, or what Lancelot referred to as the Ancient-Team from a short time ago. These were Mr. Biggs' senior citizen, hunched-over army buddies. Even the man with the cane showed up for duty.

They hobbled and stumbled over the roof until they reached his side. One looked like he might possibly faint. "Okay, kid. Lead the way," Mr. Baker said.

"It's not easy," Lancelot said.

"Never is."

"You'll have to crawl through the ventilation shaft and down four flights of stairs."

"You're wasting time, kid. Let's get to it before Biggs gets hurt!"

"Right," Lancelot said. "Right. Okay. I'll go first. Okay?"

"Can't get there if you don't," Mr. Baker said. He sounded like Mr. Biggs' brother.

"Uh. Right," Lancelot said, then crawled down the ladder, scooted ahead and turned to wait for the others. They didn't descend the ladder

74

step by step. They put their feet and hands on the outside of the ladder and slid down with blinding speed. It took about three seconds per man, so in fifteen seconds they formed a tight line, directly behind him, ready to move out.

Lancelot led the way with muffled groans and grunts following behind. They fell into Chief's office, out into the hallway, and down the stairs. He kept looking behind to make sure they hadn't collapsed or keeled over dead. But they were still hobbling along after him.

When they reached the ground-floor door, Mr. Baker drew Lancelot aside. "Look, kid. When we walk through that door, I want you to fall back and let us clean up the mess. Got that?"

Lancelot nodded, his eyes wide, and wondering, as he eyed the out of breath A-Team leaning against the wall, would they survive the next five minutes? If they didn't, he wouldn't either and neither would Mr. Biggs. As they stepped through the doorway, they could hear the same voices still arguing and demanding in that same incomprehensible language.

The A-Team advanced soundlessly down the hallway, hunched over, eyes focused on the last room. When he reached the edge of the door, Mr. Baker raised his arm and the team stopped. He signaled and the cane was passed down the line until it landed in the leader's hand. He tapped against the door so lightly that the sound was nearly undetectable.

The conversation inside the room stopped. The intruder turned his head slightly, but that was all Mr. Biggs needed. He twisted the intruder's unsuspecting arm and the weapon fell to the floor.

The A-Team rushed in while Lancelot peeked around the corner.

Mr. Baker rammed the cane into the back of the intruder's knees, another jammed down on his shoulders, and a third shoved him forward. The intruder lay flat on his face with the wind completely knocked out of him. With the cane pressed against his neck, he couldn't get up. Two men grabbed his hands, slid them behind his back while a third produced a plastic pair of handcuffs and expertly positioned them around his wrists. The team shuffled a few feet and, within seconds, his ankles were cuffed.

Lancelot never saw anything happen so fast in his entire life. And never again would he refer to these men as "ancient". They were most definitely the A-Team.

Mr. Biggs nodded his thanks to the A-Team and a whispered conference transpired in a close-knit circle.

Lancelot's focus shifted from the group of army buddies to the complaining intruder. Suddenly, he realized if he didn't sit down, he'd fall down, so he stumbled back to the decoding room with his shoulder leaning against the wall for support.

At some point, Mr. Biggs entered his room and called his name. He must have repeated it because by the time Lancelot came to, the head of security was shaking his shoulder and shouting.

Lancelot slowly looked up and raised his eyebrows. "What?" he whispered.

"Back to normal."

"Back to normal?"

"Yes. Back to normal."

Lancelot frowned as his eyes moved back and forth. "I don't

hear anything."

"No." Mr. Biggs eyed Lancelot and slowly repeated his words. "Back to normal."

"Where is everybody?"

"I called some of our off-duty guys and they came and took whatshisname away. My army buddies went home."

"Went home? You can open the door?"

"Want to see?" Mr. Biggs led the way to the front door. He entered a code and the door swung open.

Lancelot smiled for the first time since Mr. Biggs brought the first box into his office. "Why did he break into the building?"

Mr. Biggs drew his lips inside his mouth as he closed the door. "This is a major substation in the agency. A lot of information comes through here, then is rerouted to other stations. He wanted to dismantle our systems," he said, then looked at Lancelot. "Permanently."

Lancelot's mouth dropped open as his head tilted to the side. "Could he have done that?"

"For a while. Maybe he only wanted to wreck everything for a while."

"So he could do—what?"

Mr. Biggs shrugged his shoulders. "We don't know yet. May never know."

"I didn't know you knew another language?"

"Know several."

Before Lancelot could ask the next question, Mr. Biggs grabbed the master key card off his desk. And to Lancelot's utter amazement, he marched to the elevator. "Time to make my rounds," he said, then turned around. "Good work, kid. Saved the agency."

"I did?"

"Yes. Wouldn't be surprised if you got a medal or something."

"But," Lancelot said. "I was really scared."

"Doesn't matter how scared you are, kid. It's the results that count."

Lancelot opened his mouth to respond, but Mr. Biggs was already gone. He shook his head. He wasn't sure why yet, somehow, he hoped he wouldn't get a medal. As the elevator door closed, Lancelot returned to the decoding room and, with a great deal of determination, decoded the next message.

The Torn Letter

Lancelot left his house early to get a head start on the workload accumulated at his part-time job as a decoder at the intelligence agency. As he approached the front door, he walked with his head down then bumped into the mail carrier who had just dropped off the mail. "Sorry, Hal," Lancelot said. Except, it wasn't their regular mail carrier. It was someone else. Occasionally, Lancelot worked in the mornings during holidays so he knew the regular mail carrier.

"The man lowered his head, muttered something incomprehensible, turned quickly and moved on. He wore his hat low over his brow with his face averted. His walk was different from their usual mail carrier. Hal walked with that gait that came with decades of carrying a heavy load over one shoulder. This man walked evenly as someone who hadn't spent years carrying weight on one side of his body. Yet there was the slightest limp that was easily missed unless someone looked closely

Who was he? Ever curious, Lancelot studied the man as he walked away.

Now, here is where curiosity evolved into suspicion. As the mail carrier continued down the sidewalk, his pace picked up and he didn't deliver mail to any of the other buildings. While he waited to cross to the other side of the street, he nearly doubled over with a hacking series of coughs. Finally, he recovered, crossed the street, and headed down a narrow alley. Just before entering the alley, he looked over both shoulders. Had his gaze remained on Lancelot just a fraction longer than it should or was it his imagination?

Lancelot's brows drew together. He's hiding from something or someone. But why? He glanced at his watch to see if he had enough time to follow the guy but decided there must be an explanation. Most likely Hal was ill or on vacation. As impossible as it seemed, there may be a reason the other buildings had no mail today. But why did the intelligence agency receive mail along the street and no one else?

No doubt it was merely an odd series of events. Lancelot rang the buzzer then turned to face the park across the street. One squirrel chased another one up a tree. That absorbed Lancelot momentarily then he realized Mr. Biggs hadn't punched in the code to open the door, so he pressed the buzzer again.

When Lancelot stepped through the door, Mr. Biggs stood in the hallway holding the few pieces of mail the carrier had delivered.

"Not much mail today," Lancelot said.

Mr. Biggs raised puzzled eyes. "No."

"I suppose Hal is on vacation or sick or something."

"Hope that's all it is," Mr. Biggs said vaguely, then walked into his office and laid the mail on his desk.

"Hope that's all?" Lancelot said and was about to follow the head of security into his office, but the phone on Mr. Biggs' desk rang, and he answered it, pushing the small bundle of mail aside.

Lancelot's footsteps echoed down the hallway. He heard the murmur of a few voices but that was it. By the time he reached the doorway leading into the decoding room, he heard Mr. Biggs end the call so he returned to his office, "Not many people here today, Mr. Biggs."

"No, not many people here," Mr. Biggs said absently.

"Is that why you're taking care of the mail?"

"That's why," Mr. Biggs said. "No school today?"

"Teachers are at a conference, so there's no school." Mr. Biggs returned to his work so Lancelot retraced his steps and entered the decoding room. Five messages needed decoding. He peeled the top one off the pile then sat tapping his mechanical pencil on his desk as his mind settled into the intricacies of decoding.

It was unusually quiet on the ground floor, so when someone pressed the front-door buzzer, Lancelot jumped. Rarely did anyone come to the intelligence agency when much of the staff was gone. He heard Mr. Biggs step into the hallway. After he punched in the code, the door swung open.

"Hal? What are you doing here?" Mr. Biggs said.

Lancelot stepped into the hallway and observed Mr. Biggs facing the regular mail carrier.

With his mouth agape in surprise, Hal shifted his heavy mailbag. "What do you mean what am I doing here? Delivering the mail is what

81

I'm doing here. Anyway, I always get to your address about this time of day." The regular mail carrier wasn't so much insulted as surprised.

"Right. Of course, Hal. You're always here about now. Lost track of time," Mr. Biggs said, covering up his initial statement.

"Know what you mean," Hal said graciously. "Happens to me all the time." He handed over the usual large pile of mail then walked back through the door.

With eyes even more puzzled than when Lancelot first arrived, the head of security pivoted and returned to his office leaving the young decoder in the hallway wondering what happened.

Lancelot walked rapidly to Mr. Biggs' office and leaned against the doorway.

Mr. Biggs sorted through the first, small pile of mail delivered by the man impersonating a mail carrier.

Lancelot observed the mail consisted of items that were normally delivered to private homes rather than a place of business much less an intelligence agency. There was a flyer advertising a big sale at a hardware store, several flyers from pizza shops, and a small catalog from a men's clothing store just down the street. The men's clothing store catalog bulged along the midsection.

Mr. Biggs opened the catalog then hunched over a handwritten envelope shoved into the middle. Envelopes delivered to the agency are always typewritten, so why was this one handwritten? The envelope didn't have the cancellation stamp inked in wavy lines at the top, right-hand corner indicating the post office had processed it. Nothing goes through the post office without the telltale cancellation stamp at the top.

There wasn't a stamp affixed to the top corner either, so someone had never intended for the envelope to be mailed.

But those two things paled in comparison to what was written on the front. Someone had written the words, "Colonel Biggs" in large letters across the middle. Colonel? So, the head of security was once a colonel in the army. He knew Mr. Biggs was a retired army intelligence officer, but this was the first time he knew his rank. Nothing else appeared on the envelope except the name and army rank of the head of security. Not even the address of the intelligence agency.

"It's weird you got a letter with just your name on it," Lancelot said in a fishing sort of way. When no answer was forthcoming, he added, "Did you ever get mail here before?"

"No."

Mr. Biggs clasped a letter opener and used that to flip the envelope over to look at the back. It was sealed with red wax in such a manner there was absolutely no possibility anyone could open it then reseal it without being detected.

It was then that Mr. Biggs opened a drawer and pulled out a pair of plastic evidence gloves. Fingerprints? He was obviously going to check for fingerprints.

At that moment, Lancelot thought back to the man who delivered this letter. Did he wear gloves? He didn't remember but the man had to otherwise, his identity would be revealed very quickly especially at an intelligence agency where they had an entire lab devoted to analyzing evidence. He had to wear gloves unless he was a total amateur.

This envelope was so unusual, Mr. Biggs didn't want to mix his fingerprints with the person who wrote and sent this unique piece of mail. Slowly, he slit open the envelope and withdrew two pieces of paper. One piece of paper was the regular full size, but the other one was a half sheet torn top to bottom with jagged edges like a puzzle that the pieces had to fit perfectly in order to match. What was happening here? It was like a movie where two unknown people were scheduled to meet with each carrying a piece of a puzzle that must fit perfectly in order to establish trust.

As Mr. Biggs studied it with great care, Lancelot said, "Do you think the torn paper is important?"

"It's important."

Lancelot silently took half a step closer to the desk as he arched his neck trying to read the words on the letter. It wasn't easy since the letter was upside down and written in a nervous scrawl. He did recognize one word even upside down and sloppily written. And it was written with the exact same handwriting as the outside of the envelope. The letter began, "Colonel Biggs".

"Do you want something?" Mr. Biggs said.

"Uh, well I just wondered what you were doing. First, a fake mail carrier delivers something that looks, well, suspicious, then Hal shows up later with the usual mail," Lancelot said. "I mean it sounds really strange; don't you think?"

Mr. Biggs nodded slowly as he put down the magnifying glass he used. "Very strange."

Lancelot's mind raced for an excuse to stay another few minutes in case Mr. Biggs was willing to reveal what was happening. "Did you recognize the first mail carrier?"

"No, and I should have paid closer attention. When I opened the door, he remained on the next step down, so all I saw was the top of his hat. He shoved the mail into my hands and immediately turned around. Dead giveaway. My fault for not recognizing something that was obviously wrong. Figured Hal was sick or on vacation. This isn't the kind of mail we get. That should have been my second clue," Mr. Biggs said then looked up. "Did you get a good look at him?"

"Not really. His hat was pulled down and his head lowered like he did for you," Lancelot said. "It was like he didn't want me to see him. Hal always says hi, but this guy seemed to avoid me."

Mr. Biggs leaned forward in his chair. "Now, think, kid. Was there anything about him you can remember?"

Lancelot took that as an invitation to stay in his office and discuss the matter. He sat in a chair while he folded his arms and stared at the ceiling. "The hair that stuck out at the bottom of his hat was brown with gray streaks running through it."

Mr. Biggs nodded encouragingly then waited.

Lancelot closed his eyes as his mind drifted back to when he bumped into the man at the bottom of the step. "Hal's skin is tanned from being in the sun a lot. This guy was very pale like he stayed inside most of the time." He was into it now as tiny pieces of his memory rose to the surface. "We stood together a second as he hit the sidewalk and I hadn't stepped up to the first step yet. He was about two inches taller than I am, so he'd be about five feet eleven inches. He was fairly thin, too."

Lancelot opened his eyes and waited until Mr. Biggs wrote down the description. "Okay. Brown hair salted with gray, pale, about five feet eleven inches tall, and on the thin side."

"We bumped into each other and when I apologized, he just mumbled and turned away. Most people react, but he didn't. Lancelot looked up. "His breathing had a wheezing sound like the kid at school who suffers from asthma. Just before he crossed the street, he doubled over because he was coughing so hard. You know what I mean?"

"I know what you mean."

"Glasses?" Mr. Biggs said. "Did he wear glasses?"

"I don't think he did but I'm not positive."

Mr. Biggs sat back as he thought about it. "You're involved in this, because you may have to help identify the man at some point."

Lancelot leaned forward hopefully. "Well, do you think I could read what's in the letter then?"

Mr. Biggs studied the young decoder's eager face then nodded.

Lancelot rose out of his chair and stood by the desk while Mr. Biggs used the letter opener to adjust the two letters so the boy could read them.

Colonel Biggs,

You may already know that I work for Signal Defense Systems. I've worked here for twelve years now, and there's never been a problem with security.

But something strange is happening here and I don't know who I can turn to. I feel as though I can't trust anyone so I'm writing to see if you can help. We've been working on a defense system project we hope to sell to the government. It will aid in keeping our military forces much safer when they are deployed abroad especially in countries hostile to ours.

I've kept the military informed of our progress throughout the planning and testing phase. Our testing phase is nearly complete so we invited six of the top military people to observe this last phase which they are eager to do. We anticipate a large order at that time.

Here's the problem. I'm extremely careful about safeguarding my computer whenever I leave the room or leave the building at the end of the day. For the past week, it's obvious someone is trying to break into my system to retrieve the testing information on which I have worked.

In the past, there have been attempts from outsiders to hack into our computers and either steal or destroy our software, but they've been un-successful. Since they were unsuccessful at hacking into our computers from a remote position, I'm very much afraid they are trying to break into our system from within the building which seems foolish since that would be equally difficult.

No new employees have been hired in any capacity for the past year. This means, someone I know and possibly trust is willing to either sell or destroy this new defense system project.

I discussed my concerns with a colleague, but he thinks I'm imaging things. I even went to the president of the company, but he didn't believe me either for the same reason. It doesn't make sense. It's as if they're looking the other way while someone either steals or destroys a project which required four years of work to developed.

Colonel Biggs, I'm handwriting this because I don't want this letter on my computer system. I have no idea how you can help, but I have no one else to turn to.

I've scribbled a few lines on a second page then torn it in half so there are jagged edges. I've sealed the envelope in such a manner that it would be very obvious if someone opened it. The purpose of the second letter is that I do worry someone will intercept this letter. If the person who delivers this letter also presents the other half of the torn letter, you'll know the person can be trusted. However, if the other half of the torn letter is not presented, then we'll know my worst fears have been realized and it's been intercepted.

Thank you, colonel. You were a good friend to my father. I hope you'll be a good friend to me as well.

Alfred West, PhD

"But that first guy didn't give you the other half of the torn letter," Lancelot said.

"No. Obviously something happened to the person West gave this letter to. The imposter wasn't aware there was a torn letter inside the envelope and he was to present the other half as proof he was the genuine carrier. Beyond that, how did the imposter know West had written a letter and was sending it directly to me?"

"And why didn't he destroy the letter rather than deliver it to you?" Lancelot said.

"Alfred West expects to hear from me very shortly. I can only assume the imposter feared that if the letter was destroyed, West would contact me directly. But was there a private message that was supposed to be delivered with this letter? Was the original carrier supposed to tell me something?" Mr. Biggs said then an idea struck him. "And is West's office bugged? Is that how someone knew about the letter sent to me?

"Bugged? Did someone plant a listening device in his office?" Lancelot murmured.

They sat quietly immersed in their own thoughts for a moment then Lancelot said, "I don't understand what Mr. West expects you to do about this."

"It's Dr. West not Mr. West," Mr. Biggs said. "I don't understand it either," "But his father was in the army with me. Major West was a good friend of mine. I need to think about how I can help his son."

"Are you going to call Dr. West and tell him what happened?"

Mr. Biggs sat back in his chair. "Not yet. I need time to work through some things," he said then added. "You did a good job giving me some details about the imposter, kid. You might think of something else later. Let me know right away if you do."

Lancelot was being dismissed and he didn't want to be dismissed. Something was happening here, and he was on the outside of it. He rose to leave then remembered another detail. "He limped just a tiny bit."

Mr. Biggs looked up. "Limped? Do you remember which leg? Can you demonstrate how he limped?"

Lancelot closed his eyes again recalling the rhythm of the man as he walked down the sidewalk, crossed the street, and slipped into the alley. Could he imitate his walk? He stepped into the hallway and waited for Mr. Biggs to follow him. He nodded to the rhythm then stepped off on his left foot attempting to copy his exact movement.

"Right leg," Mr. Biggs said.

"Yes, right leg," Lancelot said then waited in the hallway while the head of security returned to his office.

Still wearing his evidence gloves, Mr. Biggs picked up the two pieces of paper and the envelope and headed for the elevator with Lancelot tailing behind him. When the head of security stepped through the open elevator door, his eyebrows rose as Lancelot stood beside him. "All right," Mr. Biggs said. "You can go to the lab with me since you're a witness." He took his phone out of his pocket and punched in a number. "Chief, got a private letter addressed to me from Major West's son. I'm headed to the lab to get fingerprints. I'll keep you posted on it."

This was serious business, so Lancelot hid an excited smile since he'd never been in the lab where all sorts of evidence was analyzed. When they walked into the laboratory, two people were busy at work. A woman, who sat at a desk, looked up and nodded. A man who looked like he was old enough to retire was at the far end of the room.

"Got something for us to work on, Biggs?" Mike said. "We've got an emergency request right now. Can it wait till tomorrow?"

Mr. Biggs drew in his lips for a second then said, "Just fingerprints. I can take care of the process part of it if you don't mind, Mike."

"Don't mind at all," Mike said. "Are you checking for fingerprints on the paper samples you brought with you?"

"That's right," Mr. Biggs said.

"Well, if you need ninhydrin, it's on the shelf right behind you," Mike said then returned to his work.

"Thanks," Mr. Biggs said, then allowed his finger to drift along the

90

bottles on the shelf until he found the label that read ninhydrin. He pulled it from the shelf and sat at a table, signaling Lancelot to sit beside him. Sensing the boy wanted to ask a question, the head of security held up his hand and began to explain. "You can't see any fingerprints on the two paper samples or the envelope, right?" he said in a low voice so as not to disturb the others.

Lancelot shook his head. "Can't see a thing," he whispered.

"Okay. Visible fingerprints are called patent prints. When the fingerprints are invisible, they are called latent prints. Everybody has a certain amount of sweat or oil on their skin which is transferred to something they may touch. Unless the person or persons who touched these paper samples wore gloves, there are going to be fingerprints on them. When he handed me this mail, I would have noticed if he wore gloves, and he didn't. We'd expect to find West's prints and those of the person he originally sent to deliver the letter. But I'm interested in finding the fingerprints of the man impersonating the mail carrier.

"Right. I get that," Lancelot said. "And because I can't see any prints, they're latent prints, right?"

"Right. Now, paper is a porous material," Mr. Biggs said, lifting his eyebrows to see if Lancelot was following him.

"I understand what porous means. Paper has tiny, microscopic holes in it."

Mr. Biggs nodded then continued. "After I apply ninhydrin, I use a steam iron to bring out the color purple. The purple highlights the fingerprints. After it turns purples, I photograph it."

"Then you have to match the fingerprint to a specific person?"

"Right," Mr. Biggs. "I can do this part of it, but Mike matches fingerprints we collect here to fingerprints the FBI keeps on its database."

The head of security applied the ninhydrin reagent to both sheets of paper and the envelope. He added water to a steam iron, allowed it to heat to a certain temperature, then ironed the two sheets of paper and the envelope.

A slow smile crept onto Lancelot's face as he watched invisible fingerprints turn purple. "That's incredible!" he said, nearly forgetting to whisper.

Mr. Biggs smiled ruefully, appreciating the young decoder's enthusiasm. "Have to photograph them now," he said briskly. He glanced at the clock as he moved silently to the table where the fingerprints were photographed. After completing that step in the process, he said, "Wait here, kid. I need to talk to Mike and tell him the situation. Maybe he can give this priority." He gathered the photographs, the two sheets of paper and envelope, and headed to the opposite end of the lab. He spoke quietly to Mike then handed the evidence to him.

Mike adjusted his glasses and read the two sheets of paper as well as the photographs while the brows on his forehead deepened with every paragraph he read. Drawing a deep breath, he looked up at Mr. Biggs and nodded. "I'll take care of this today."

Mr. Biggs nodded gratefully, turned on his heel, and walked out the door with Lancelot directly behind him.

"Will we find out who it is today?" Lancelot said.

"Maybe. Maybe not. Depends on whether the fingerprints show up on the FBI database."

"If the fingerprints aren't in their files, we won't know who it is."

"Right, we won't know who it is," Mr. Biggs said.

Lancelot waited for the elevator to arrive beside a distracted Mr. Biggs. "How many fingerprints does the FBI have in its database?"

"Seventy million fingerprints last I heard. Probably more now."

"Wow! That's a lot of prints."

"It is," Mr. Biggs said. "But it's not enough prints if our guy's prints don't match anything the FBI has."

"I know," Lancelot said softly.

Suddenly, the sound of a piercing alarm rang through the hallway. An even more piercing voice came on the PA system. "Evacuate the building immediately! All personnel evacuate the building immediately! Stairway only! Stairway only!"

Lancelot stood stunned. This hadn't happened in the entire time he'd worked at the intelligence agency and he froze.

Mr. Biggs grabbed the boy's arm and led him quickly down the hallway where a handful of people headed for the stairway. "Watch your step, kid," he said as Lancelot began to stumble.

Halfway to the ground floor, Lancelot's sense of balance returned and Mr. Biggs released his arm.

The backdoor was programmed to unlock automatically when the alarm went off. Some of the employees were already filing out of the building creating small groups of twos and threes in the rear parking lot.

Lancelot's legs were steadier, but his mind still felt a bit numb. The shrilling alarm and instructions to evacuate the building by way of the stairway had unsettled him. What could possibly have happened? Was it a bomb or some object that was discovered and couldn't be identified or accounted for? There was no odor of smoke in the air. In any case, if there was a fire, they'd hear fire sirens wailing.

Except for those in charge of investigating the cause of the alarm, Chief was the last to leave the building. He walked to the far side of the parking lot then his eyes scanned the area looking for someone. When his eyes fell on Mr. Biggs, he signaled for him. Mr. Biggs stepped away from Lancelot and joined Chief.

Lancelot wasn't a lipreader, but he thought he read Alfred West's name spoken. Mr. Biggs was briefing Chief on what happened that morning. Chief listened attentively drawing his brows together and nodding his head occasionally. Mr. Biggs' phone call alerted the Chief about the letter, but he hadn't known about the imposter posing as the mail carrier or the contents of the letter. Eventually, Mr. Biggs briefing of the situation ended and Chief began to speak.

Even in the brief time Lancelot had been with the intelligence agency, it was obvious Chief and Mr. Biggs had known each other a long time. It was rumored that Chief was also in army intelligence and Mr. Biggs reported directly to him. The head of security enjoyed freedom and privileges granted to no one else in the entire building. It wasn't the first time he wondered what Mr. Biggs' position at the intelligence agency was beyond that of the head of security. Lancelot's eyes slowly studied each group but not one single person looked at Chief and Mr. Biggs. Obviously, they were accustomed to this.

Lancelot returned his focus to the two men again and tried unsuccessfully to read their lips. They had shifted their position, so he gave up on that. No one else seemed worried or concerned about this but his mind felt the need to sit down in a quiet area and regain momentum. His eyes wandered around the parking lot and came to rest on Mr. Biggs' beat up, rusted out truck. Perhaps the head of security wouldn't object if he used this to isolate himself from everyone else for a few moments.

Lancelot's first attempt to open the truck door failed miserably. It didn't appear to be locked, so he put a little extra zeal into the effort. It opened but not without squeaking the entire way. He looked over his shoulder expecting all eyes to be on him. Not so much as a single person glimpsed his way. Sliding onto the ragged seat, he closed the door as quietly as possible then leaned his head back on the crumbling headrest and allowed his eyes to close.

Within thirty seconds, Lancelot heard something so quiet, had he taken a deep breath he would have missed it. Even though it was an old rattly truck, it was wonderfully quiet inside when the engine wasn't coughing and belching. His brows drew together and he opened his eyes. He noticed a thin catalog from a local upscale men's store laying on the floor of the driver's side of the truck. He couldn't imagine Mr. Biggs ever shopping at a place like that.

Lancelot's eyes grew wider and he sat bolt upright. He'd seen a catalog just like that thirty minutes earlier. The imposter, pretending to be a mail carrier, had delivered it with the letter for Mr. Biggs stuffed in the middle. He wasn't sure why, but suddenly the two identical catalogs and the piercing sound of the alarm that drove all of them out into the parking lot formed a unit of evidence.

Lancelot shoved open the door then, with long purposeful strides, headed in the direction of Mr. Biggs and Chief. As he grew nearer, he noticed Chief on his phone, his brows drawing closer together as he listened intently to what the caller was saying. As he spoke, he glanced repeatedly at the head of security.

Chief shoved the phone into his side pocket while he related the essence of the conversation to the head of security.

Mr. Biggs' face grew as solemn as it ever did as Chief continued to discuss the phone call. He nodded then drew his hand across his chin while he processed the information. Out of the corner of his eye, he spotted Lancelot approaching and held up his hand to stop the conversation. Both men turned with quizzical looks on their faces. The young decoder never hurried. His movements were usually measured in a haphazard sort of way, yet he nearly broke into a trot as he hurried to reach them.

Once Lancelot reached their side, he grew hesitant. Was he wrong, and they'd think he was silly or stupid?

Sensing the problem, Mr. Biggs placed his hand on Lancelot's shoulder. "What is it, kid?"

"Well, it's probably nothing," Lancelot began in a rush.

"Just tell us and we'll decide," Chief said encouragingly.

"I remembered the letter was tucked inside a men's clothing catalog." When both men nodded, Lancelot continued. "Well, I wanted to sit down in a quiet place, so I sat in your truck. Hope you don't mind."

"I don't mind. Just tell us what happened."

"I closed my eyes but then I heard this tiny sound. It almost sounded like a soda can being opened, except the sound was so soft, if I'd been taking a breath, I would have missed it. I opened my eyes and looked down. On the floor, shoved up so far I hadn't really noticed it, was a men's clothing catalog. It looked exactly like the one where you found the torn letter."

Mr. Biggs and Chief exchanged looks. That's when Lancelot knew he had been right to report the incident immediately after it happened.

"You did the right thing in reporting this," Mr. Biggs said, patting him on the shoulder.

Chief called the security team inside and informed them that there was a catalog inside Biggs' truck that was identical to the one delivered to the agency earlier in the morning. A few sentences were exchanged and the call ended.

Seconds later, two men attired in protective gear came through the backdoor with a container in hand. They placed the catalog in the container then proceeded to search the entire truck front to back. They disappeared back into the building while Lancelot wondered where they'd take both catalogs and what they'd find. Secretly, he hoped they'd find something or he'd feel like a total alarmist.

Thirty minutes later, someone came to the backdoor and gave the all-clear signal for everyone to return to the building. Chief raised his hand and beckoned the man. When the man arrived, he said, "Any preliminary information on what set off the alarm?"

"Both catalogs hid a small, flat device set to spew toxic material into the air," he said. "We don't know exactly what the toxic material is yet, but that's the preliminary report. We're taking both catalogs to headquarters where the lab has equipment to specifically identify toxic material. Hopefully, we'll know more later today."

Chief nodded and the man rushed back into the building to join the group who were nearly ready to leave for headquarters.

Lancelot listened to the conversation between Chief and Mr. Biggs as he quietly trailed behind them into the building.

"Look, Chief," Mr. Biggs began. "I need to go to Signal Defense Systems disguised as someone from the military authorized to evaluate the test results. They're expecting someone from the military so everyone will be expecting military personnel. I have to get inside the building for a period of time and it's the only way I can do that without raising suspicion. You can't send someone who doesn't know anything about defense systems."

Chief nodded as he studied the ground in front of his feet. "Right. I know you'll have to go, but someone has attempted to take your life in the past thirty minutes," he said then looked pointedly at Mr. Biggs. "Twice. Once in your office and, if that failed to take you out, they placed the same deadly device in your truck which was set to go off by the vibration of the door opening and closing. It didn't take long for the team to evaluate what happened and evacuate the building just to be safe. What they put in your truck has to be the same toxic gas that was in your office. The one in your office had a timer attached to it. I suppose the one they placed inside the truck was set to go with vibration since they couldn't know when you'd leave the building." He sighed and shook his head. "I don't know what we would have told Lancelot's parents if he hadn't left the truck immediately."

"I thought of that, too." Mr. Biggs sighed.

"No explosion, so whoever planted it inside those two men's catalogs, only wanted to take you out, not the entire building," Chief said. "Fortunately, you had left your office to go to the lab when the timer went off and the toxic material was dispersed. At least the alarm system picked it up and the building was cleared before it had a chance to spread any farther."

"I was lucky," Mr. Biggs said. "One of the issues is the person who delivered the torn letter and catalog may work at Signal Defense Systems. If he does, he'll recognize me. The problem is, I won't recognize him."

"But Lancelot probably would," Chief said.

"Probably."

"Can't put him in that kind of danger," Chief said.

"Right. Too dangerous for the kid."

"I'll go," Lancelot called ahead. "I'm sure I'd recognize that guy. I'll pretend to be, uh," he said then a stroke of genius hit. "I'll pretend to be your grandson."

Both men turned around and studied the young decoder with two conflicting thoughts. Has this kid completely lost his mind followed quickly by that's the only way we can possibly discover the identity of the man who delivered the letter and the catalogs which held the poisonous gas.

Lancelot's thoughts followed along the same lines. He had to be absolutely insane to volunteer for this job. Yet, he was the only one who could identify the man. Not knowing quite how to react, he said,

"Should I go home and change?"

"What if the guy who delivered the letter is only a courier and doesn't really work at Signal Defense Systems?" Mr. Biggs said.

"Then Lancelot would be at risk for nothing," Chief said.

"But you won't know that until we get there," Lancelot said.

Both men nodded. Couldn't argue that point. The men pivoted and walked rapidly into the building with Lancelot close behind. Inside the building, they took the elevator to the fourth floor. While the elevator rose, the two men studied the fourteen-year-old decoder who suddenly found his shoes intensely interesting.

Chief sat at his desk while the other two sat in chairs across from him. "Bake," he said. When Mr. Biggs nodded knowingly, Chief punched in a number. "Bake? Chief here. Look, we need an army car and driver dressed in military uniform out back in…" he glanced at Mr. Biggs who mouthed the words forty-five minutes. "Forty-five minutes. Think you can manage that? Good! Thanks, Bake."

Lancelot had met Mr. Biggs' army buddy, Mr. Baker, several times. The first time was when they rescued an agent, Kat Stephens, being held prisoner in a safehouse. Another time, Mr. Baker's team prevented an agency traitor and two foreign agents from escaping with classified material. The last time he saw Mr. Baker was the day there was an intruder in the building and he picked up a container with a suspected bomb inside. He liked and trusted Mr. Baker and, right now, they needed someone who was thoroughly reliable. Lancelot looked up as Chief discontinued the call.

"You will need a uniform," Chief said.

"Got one at home. If Jim is free, he can collect it for me."

Chief pressed a button and asked him to step into the office.

Jim tapped on the door then slipped inside. Mr. Biggs stood, handed him the key to his house then said, "My uniform is in the hall closet. Get it for me, will you, Jim?"

"Yes, sir," Jim said then turned on his heel and left. They could hear him heading for the stairway rather than taking the slower elevator. Everyone was in a raging hurry because they had no idea of the imposter's identity, if he was employed by Signal Defense Systems, or if he was in the process of leaving the country.

"We need someone to call Signal Defense Systems and inform them a military representative will be there within two hours to observe the tests they are conducing," Mr. Biggs said.

Chief thought a moment. "General Bergman. He's still active military and helped us once before."

"Right. Good choice."

Lancelot's head swiveled back and forth between Chief and Mr. Biggs. They developed this unique strategy with lightning-fast efficiency. It was as if they'd done this one hundred times before when they were in army intelligence together. He sat back in his chair and realized that's why they could pull a plan together this quickly. They had so much experience doing just what they were doing now over a thirty-year period.

They appeared to be equals planning a mission rather than the head of security speaking with deference to the head of the intelligence agency. Not for the first time, Lancelot wondered who Mr. Biggs was?

After making the call, Chief removed his glasses and squeezed the bridge of his nose between his thumb and index finger. "Bergman said he'd arrange it so Signal Defense Systems knows someone is coming and to give that person every courtesy." Then he shifted his focused to Lancelot. "You look about as unthreatening as anyone could hope for but we need to find another t-shirt for you. It needs to be something that will draw people's attention away from your face so all they see is the shirt. You need a baseball cap, too."

"Okay. I mean I understand, sir. Should I run home and see what I can find?"

"No, we'll dig up something for you here."

"I have t-shirts," Mr. Biggs said. "They'll be big, but that's all the more distracting."

"I want you to return to the decoding room and at least try to get some work done," Chief said. "There are a few things I want to discuss with Goliath, I mean Biggs."

"Yes, sir," Lancelot said then reluctantly left the room. Goliath. He'd heard Mr. Biggs referred to as Goliath several times before. Was it a code name or something else? As he took the elevator to the ground floor, he wondered what they were discussing that they didn't want him to hear. He was part of the team, why couldn't he stay? When he reached the decoding room, he sighed then sat at his desk and placed a message that needed to be decoded on his desk. His eyes drifted to the dent in the wall in front of him while he twirled his mechanical pencil between his index and middle fingers. In a surprisingly short period of time, he heard Mr. Biggs step into his office.

Within a minute, he stood in the doorway with three t-shirts draped over his arm and a baseball cap in his hand. "Wear whichever shirt you hate the least, kid. The goal is to draw everyone's eyes away from your face. And don't forget to take the baseball cap with you when we leave. Normally, you'd take your hat off when you entered a facility. But, this time, you'll need to keep it on. Okay?"

"Right." As Lancelot inspected the t-shirts, his mouth turned down at the corners. He was far from a clothes horse, but these were wildly colored neon shirts in every imaginable color. No doubt about it. Everyone would stare at the t-shirt and not his face. Mr. Biggs must have worn these various times for the same reason. He wanted to draw attention to the shirts and away from him.

When the backdoor buzzer rang, Mr. Biggs walked past the decoding room without looking in. He thanked Jim for picking up his uniform then spent the next ten minutes changing behind a closed door.

While Mr. Biggs changed into his uniform, Lancelot slipped on a neon t-shirt. He stood when he heard the head of security heading his way. This time he stopped at his doorway. "Let's meet Bake in the rear parking lot. Knowing, Bake, he's probably already there and waiting for us."

It took Lancelot a moment to stop gawking. The ribbons plastered over the left side of Colonel Biggs' uniform were incredible. There must be a dozen of them at least. The transformation from the head of security to a colonel in the army was staggering. His bearing was different. He stood straighter, his shoulders more squared off, and he had an air of authority. The disguise was perfect. Had Lancelot passed Mr. Biggs on the sidewalk, he wouldn't have recognized him, and he worked with him three days after school each week. Today was an exception since school was closed for a teacher's conference. This was perfect. If he couldn't recognize Mr. Biggs neither would the man posing as a mail carrier.

"Come on, kid. Let's go," Colonel Biggs said.

"Oh, right," Lancelot said then marched behind the colonel, down the hallway, and out the backdoor where a car was parked that looked very much like a military vehicle. "Mr. Baker is here already. And he's wearing an army uniform, too."

"I figured he'd be here," Colonel Biggs said crisply. "And I knew he'd be in uniform. You need to refer to him as Sergeant Baker or just sergeant once we're at Signal Defense Systems."

"Sergeant Baker," Lancelot said. "Okay, I'll remember."

As soon as the two headed in Sergeant Baker's direction, he climbed out of the driver's seat and held the backdoor open.

"Thank you, sergeant," Colonel. Biggs said.

Sergeant Baker saluted while standing at attention and said, "Colonel."

The colonel climbed into the backseat while Lancelot walked around to the other side and slipped in beside him. Once they were in place, Sergeant Baker quietly closed the backdoor then slid behind the wheel.

"Do you know where Signal Defense Systems is, sergeant?"

"Yes, sir. General Bergman called and briefed me on it. We'll be there in fifteen minutes."

"Good," Colonel Biggs said, then sat back and silently looked out the side window. Halfway to their destination, he picked up his phone and punched in a number. "Mike? Any information on the fingerprints yet? Okay. Let me know as soon as you find out." After that, there was silence until they reached Signal Defense Systems.

It was a reverse performance once Sergeant Baker parked the car. He opened the backdoor for the colonel who slowly, and with dignity befitting a colonel in the army, got out of the car.

Lancelot's neon, oversized shirt billowed as he walked then he remembered to pull down his baseball cap. His hair stuck out a bit but that added to the impression that he was an unthreatening teenager tagging along after his grandfather. He walked around the car as the colonel led the way with his sergeant a step behind and the colonel's grandson dragging his feet behind the sergeant.

"Wander around the front part of the building and see what you can pick up, sergeant," Colonel Biggs said under his breath. He used a hand signal to draw Lancelot to his side. "Look, kid, keep your head down and your eyes and ears open. Follow me from a distance. If there's something you want to show or tell me, clear your throat. Okay?"

"Okay," Lancelot said softly, then lowered his head and pulled down the brim of his baseball cap even farther on his head. As his hands grew increasingly moist, he wondered how insane this idea was relative to his other ideas. Fairly close to the top, he decided.

They were forty feet from the front door when it opened and three people came forward. The man in front extended his arm and shook hands with Colonel Biggs while glancing at the young man who stood at his side staring at the ground as if he were already suffering from extreme boredom before he walked through the door.

"My grandson," Colonel Biggs explained. "Visiting, so I brought him along. Hope you don't mind," he said, knowing the need for this government contract was so great, they wouldn't object to bringing anyone along.

"No problem at all, colonel. I'm Alfred West, head of research and development."

Lancelot studied the man who wrote the letter asking for help. Yet, he seemed rather calm. The only thing that gave him away was an occasional nervous twitch in his right eye. I wonder if he knows the other half of the torn letter wasn't presented at the same time as the envelope. Who had the other half of the letter and what happened to him? Perhaps Alfred West already knew the other half wasn't delivered and that was the reason for the nervous twitch. In fact, he had to know, because the person assigned to give them the other half of the torn letter would have reported back to Dr. West. When the messenger failed to report, he knew something had gone awry.

Lancelot sensed movement from a window. Someone within the building peeked through the blinds then quickly stepped back. Was that just curiosity or something else?

Sergeant Baker faded into the background as the representatives of Signal Defense Systems led the way down the hall.

"Well," Dr. West said. "We're certainly glad you came, but it was rather short notice, so I can show you videos of our latest experiments, but it wasn't possible to set up something to actually demonstrate it."

"That's fine," Colonel Biggs said. "I understand. Short notice."

As they moved down the hallway, Lancelot peered through the glass windows into the various rooms. Nothing seemed out of place. Everyone was working on something. He fell farther back from the group to gain perspective of the rooms and how they positioned themselves along the hallway. He studied faces within each room, but there was nothing familiar about any of them.

Lancelot stopped briefly at one window. There was a man and a woman working at computers. Sensing someone's eyes were upon him, the man looked up. His eyes narrowed and he reached for the phone. Lancelot quickly moved on. After that, he studied people through each window from the opposite side of the hallway.

While the decoder peered through the window, the man posing as a mail carrier passed him in the hallway. And that caused a shift in plans.

The imposter now had another opportunity to end the life of Biggs. He'd been told the former army intelligence officer may prove dangerous if Major West's son, who happened to be head of research and development, was to experience and unfortunate accident.. His orders were to get rid of Biggs first followed by Dr. Alfred West. After that, his escape plan was up to him. His carefully laid plans to dispose of Colonel Biggs had failed. The imposter's only hope of survival was to eliminate the kid who was the only person alive who could identify him.

The others had rounded the corner and entered a room. By the time Lancelot reached that room, they were well into the heart of the video. He tentatively tried the doorknob, but it was locked. The video of the defense system being demonstrated was classified. Although they didn't object to Colonel Biggs' grandson being in the building, they wouldn't want him to view the video.

By now, Lancelot suspected the colonel had informed Dr. West of the attempt on his life both in his office at the agency and in the truck. He also felt sure that Dr. West knew Lancelot's sole purpose in being here was to identify the imposter posing as a mail carrier.

Blinds blocked the view from anyone casually walking by the room, but there was a tiny slit between two of the blinds. Lancelot leaned his elbows on the windowsill then crouched down to study each person. All of them had their backs to the window which didn't help with recognition. Ten people were seated in two rows watching the video. After several minutes, he straightened and stretched his back, then checked up and down the hallway for anyone who may be observing his odd behavior.

Lancelot leaned his elbows against the windowsill again and crouched in the same position as before but his neck grew tired of the angle it had held for several minutes. Drawing a deep breath, he was about to stretch once again when someone seated at the end of the second row whispered to the woman next to him. She nodded and the man stood. As soon as he turned around, Lancelot recognized him. It was the imposter he'd seen earlier that day posing as the mail carrier. He wasn't coughing at the present and was dressed completely differently. Yet there was no mistaking that he was the one.

The man took two steps towards the door then looked over his shoulder. The name printed on his white lab coat was "Simpson". While he kept an eye on the rest of the group, he slipped something out of an inner pocket. It was a manilla colored envelope which he placed on a chair before proceeding to the door. Nobody saw or heard him. Worse yet, no one suspected him. Because had Dr. West suspected this man, he would have turned him over to the company's internal security team.

Lancelot was the only one in possession of this knowledge. What if the manilla-colored envelope contained the same toxic material he'd planted in Mr. Biggs' office and truck? Everyone inside that viewing room would be badly hurt or worse.

He had to do something. But what? When the imposter was two steps from the door, inspiration struck. Lancelot wouldn't be able to hold him off indefinitely, but what he needed was to draw everyone's attention away from the video to the back of the room.

Lancelot pressed the full weight of his body against the door. As soon as Simpson tried to open it, he knew someone was on the other side attempting to block it. He looked over his shoulder again. No one from the group heard his failed attempt to open the door. Then, with one mighty shove, he overcame the boy's strength.

Lancelot flew backwards and fell against the opposite wall. The breath was knocked out of him momentarily. Even then, he shouted, "He's the one!"

While everyone else in the room turned around; Colonel Biggs leaped out of his chair and ran into the hallway.

"It's him!" Lancelot said, trying to regain his breath. "He's the one who delivered the envelope!"

"Are you all right?" Colonel Biggs said.

"Yes." Lancelot placed his hand over his chest and inhaled several times. "He laid an envelope on the chair in the back row!"

Dr. West immediately checked to see who was missing. "It's Simpson. I'll call security," he said, attempting to control his voice, then closed the door after making sure the room was clear of personnel.

"Your job is done. Go sit in the car, lock it, and wait," Colonel Biggs said then nodded at Sergeant Baker who handed the decoder the car keys so he could unlock the military vehicle. The colonel turned away and hurried down the hallway. "West, check to see if Simpson's car is in the parking lot!" he called over his shoulder. "If it isn't, alert security that he took his car and left!"

Lancelot was reluctant to leave when he could help, but he made his way down the hall amidst the intense room-by-room search that was taking place. He unlocked the car, slid onto the front seat on the passenger side, but he failed to lock the door. That failure would cost him dearly. Sighing, he leaned back on the headrest but kept his eyes focused on the front door of the building.

Suddenly, the backdoor of the car flew open, and someone slipped inside. "Start the car and let's get out of here." It was the voice he remembered from that morning. "Don't turn around. Just start the car and head for the exit."

"Well, uh I'm only fourteen. I've never driven a c-car before," he lied convincingly.

"Don't make me repeat myself!" Simpson said, his voice shifting from reasonable to threatening. He had ducked down so only his eyes showed above the backseat.

"Okay," Lancelot said with a voice that was none too steady. He scooted over to the driver's side. The only time he'd driven a car was when he and Mr. Biggs rescued Kat Stephens from foreign agents trying to capture her and he'd wrecked that car beyond repair. But, this car was slightly different and, in his anxious state of mind, his eyes flew over the dashboard but saw nothing that looked even remotely familiar. He sat for fifteen seconds trying to remember the sequenced he used before to start a car but his mind was an absolute blank.

"Hurry up!"

"Right, right, I'm trying!" He may not be sure what to do but he at least needed to prove he was making an effort. He searched more carefully and pressed a button and was rewarded or doomed to hear the engine start. At that moment, it occurred to Lancelot that Simpson was not wearing a seatbelt. While his left hand slowly drew his seatbelt over his shoulder and locked it in place, his right foot pressed down on the accelerator and revved the engine which muffled the locking sound of the seatbelt.

"All right! Get us out of here before they realize I'm not in the building!"

"How did you get out?"

"Window. Windows on the ground level are sealed. I unsealed one last week in case I needed it." He coughed several times then recovered.

But would anyone think to look for that? Lancelot heard that note of pride in Simpson's voice. An old saying came to mind, "Pride goes before a fall." He put the car in gear, pressed on the accelerator, and the car leaped forward.

"If you're trying to throw me off balance, it won't work. Now, head for the exit and turn left."

Lancelot moistened his lips as they reached the exit. He eased down on the brake not coming to a full stop until the car reached the middle of the road.

"Left! Turn left and hurry up!" Simpson said, poking him in the shoulder then checking out the back window to see if anyone had come out of the building.

Lancelot rubbed his shoulder wondering what he held in his hand. Swallowing hard, he turned left nearly ending in the ditch before he adjusted his position so the car was heading down the center of the right side of the road.

Colonel Biggs, Sergeant Baker, and he had arrived at Signal Defense Systems driving from the opposite direction. He'd never been beyond this point on the road before and didn't know what to expect. He had no idea whether, at some point, it might be possible to throw the imposter off balance. "Uh, how far are we going?"

"You don't need to know that. I'll tell you when to pull over." Simpson raised his head just enough so Lancelot could see the top half of his face in the rearview mirror.

Suddenly, he yanked the baseball cap off Lancelot's head and jammed it down over his forehead as far as it would go. If Lancelot ever got that cap back, he would immediately build a huge bonfire and toss it into the middle of it.

Now, Simpson rose higher so Lancelot could see his entire face. It was deeply lined and pale as if he spent little time outside. His was a harsh face with not an ounce of pity reflected in it. Lancelot knew if he didn't produce a plan very soon, he may not have a future.

Everyone gathered around Colonel Biggs and reported negative findings. "He must have gotten outside somehow," he said. "West, did security check to see if Simpson's car is still in the parking lot?"

"It's still there," Dr. West said.

Then a thought struck Colonel Biggs so powerfully, he noticeably paled.

"What is it, sir?" Sergeant Baker said.

"Lancelot. I told him to wait in the car."

Everyone immediately drew the same conclusion and rushed to the front door.

"The car is gone. Simpson's taken Lancelot prisoner," Colonel Biggs said, trying to maintain control of his voice. Accustomed to emergencies, his mind rapidly went through possible solutions. "Airport. There's a small airport not far from here. There may be a small plane waiting to take him out of the area."

"You're probably right, sir," Sergeant Baker said. "It's only about fifteen miles from here."

"West, do you have your car keys on you?"

Dr. West dug them out of his pocket and handed them to the colonel. "It's the dark blue one over there," he said, pointing to the car's position.

"Thanks," Colonel Biggs said as he sprinted to the car with Sergeant Baker directly behind him. "You drive," he said, tossing the keys to the sergeant.

Sergeant Baker wheeled out of the parking lot then spun the tires as he shot down the road in the direction of the small airport. "I wonder how much of a head start they have."

"Too much," Colonel Biggs said with a tight voice. "I hope I'm right about where he's taking the kid."

"Faster!" Simpson said. "By now, they're bound to figure out what happened!"

Lancelot was driving at a terrifying fifty miles per hour as it was. He was constantly taking one hand off the steering wheel and wiping it on his neon shirt. Cautiously, he pressed down on the accelerator hoping the very thing Simpson worried about would happen before they reached their destination. Every few seconds, he peered at his rearview mirror without turning his head. The road behind him was discouragingly empty. If he only knew where they were going and how much time he had to come up with a plan, at this point, any plan.

Sergeant Baker rapidly increased his speed until they were racing down the road at eighty miles per hour. He jammed on the brakes at turns then continued at the high rate of speed. Both men searched ahead hoping to find and catch up with the car holding the young decoder.

The colonel's phone buzzed. It was Mike from the lab. "Mike? What have you got for me?"

"His name is Thomas Simpson. Works for Signal Defense Systems. Just renewed his passport last month. Might be headed somewhere out of the country. There are two more prints. One of them is Alfred West, head of research and development at Signal Defense Systems. The third set of fingerprints is so smudged it's impossible to find a match on the FBI database."

"Good work. Thankfully, he didn't wear gloves. Thanks, Mike!" Colonel Biggs said. When the call ended, his eyes focused on the road ahead. "There!" he pointed to a dot on the horizon. "That's it."

Sergeant Baker increased his speed until they were less than a football field away.

"Just where are we g-going?" Lancelot said.

"I'll be there in five minutes, so don't worry about it."

It didn't escape Lancelot's notice that Simpson used the pronoun 'I' rather than 'We'. At some point between here and their destination, Simpson would no longer need him, and he'd be history. His eyes darted to the rearview mirror, and he saw a car in the distance. His focus dropped and he noticed Simpson was checking his watch. Slowly, he let up on the accelerator until it drifted back to fifty-five, although to him, it seemed as though they were still flying down the road at top speed.

Simpson coughed then looked anxiously at his watch again.

Why was he checking his watch? Was there a schedule that had to be kept by a certain time? Then it dawned on Lancelot. They could never get very far in this car. Eventually, air support would be called in, the police would be brought in, and road blocks set up. This guy wasn't stupid. He knew that, so there must be a train or plane up ahead that he had to catch. The more he thought about it the more he knew it couldn't be a train. Trains can be stopped in emergencies and checked. With airplanes, it's not that easy.

Lancelot wasn't aware of an airport in this part of the county but there must be a small airport. It had to be that. It was a conspiracy and people were waiting for him on the other end. Colonel Biggs was still alive. He'd been the target and this man had bungled it. The men's catalogs had been discovered in Colonel Biggs' office and his truck. His final attempt to end the colonel's life was a few minutes ago at Signal Defense Systems. That ended in failure as well.

Even though this man hadn't completed his assignment, there were people at the airport waiting to take him away because if they didn't, he'd be arrested, reveal names, dates, and places then the entire group of conspirators would be brought in.

The car had drawn much closer and was flashing its lights. Since it was daylight, Lancelot wouldn't have noticed had he not been looking in the rearview mirror. It had to be Colonel Biggs and Sergeant Baker, and they understood Lancelot was inside the car. They must have realized he was actually driving the car. If he made his move now, somebody would be there to take over. What he needed was for Simpson to experience just one more coughing spell. Thirty seconds later, he got his wish.

Simpson doubled over and coughed.

With that, Lancelot slammed down hard on the brakes throwing himself against the seatbelt and Simpson onto the floor. He kept pressing until the car came to a complete standstill, then shoved the gear into park, and opened the door. He tripped and fell then used the car door to pull himself upright before he staggered to the car behind him.

Colonel Biggs jumped out of the car before it came to a full stop and ran ahead. "Are you all right?" he said for the second time in thirty minutes.

"I had to drive that car!" Lancelot said, completely out of breath.

Colonel Biggs smiled briefly then said, "Stay here." He and Sergeant Baker trotted to the car ahead of them and opened the backdoor.

Simpson was a planner, not a fighter. He pulled himself off the floor and climbed out of the car defeat evident in the slump of his shoulders.

A car carrying four security people from Signal Defense Systems arrived a moment later and took custody of Thomas Simpson.

Twenty minutes later, the three sat in Dr. West's office with the door closed. Lancelot leaned back on the couch, while the colonel and sergeant sat across from Dr. West's desk. He half listened as the three men reviewed what had happened.

"Who had the other half of the torn letter?" Colonel Biggs said.

Dr. West sighed as he shook his head. "My assistant. I don't know where he is. I haven't seen him since early this morning when I gave him the envelope and his half of the torn letter. When he didn't return, I grew worried. Later, I became suspicious. He has been with me for ten years. I have no idea where he is. I tried calling him countless times. Did he willingly give Simpson the letter but forgot to give him the other half of the torn letter? Was it taken from him by force and he's now a prisoner or worse? At this point, I need to bring in the authorities."

There was a tap on the door. Dr. West looked up. "I told everyone I was not to be disturbed," he said then raised his voice. "Come in."

"Sorry sir," a young man said. "Hospital is on the phone. They think it's possible they have one of our employees in the Emergency Room. He has a concussion, but he keeps repeating "Signal Defense Systems"."

"It has to be my assistant. And all morning I thought..." Dr. West rose from his chair with a look of guilt written on his face. "I must go and see him immediately."

"We're done here," Colonel Biggs said, leading the way out the door.

Their job completed, the two men and the young decoder headed for the parking lot. As they stood at the open car door, Colonel Biggs took off his coat and hat then loosened his tie as the sergeant did the same. They tossed them in the backseat beside Lancelot.

"Where did you get this car, Bake?" Mr. Biggs said.

"Oh, you know how it is, Biggs. Called one of our active-duty buddies and he knew somebody. Didn't take more than two minutes to find the right person. No problem at all. You'll never believe who I finally talked to."

In the backseat, a slow smile spread across Lancelot's face as he listened to two people who'd known each other for decades reliving memories of another time in their lives.

~The End~

www.ingramcontent.com/pod-product-compliance
Lightning Source LLC
Chambersburg PA
CBHW071006120726
47910CB00004B/1413